# Find You in Paris

*(The Darcy Brothers)*
Alix Nichols

**Other books by Alix Nichols:**

***The Darcy Brothers:***

Raphael's Fling

***La Bohème:***

You're the One

Winter's Gift

What If It's Love?

Falling for Emma

Under My Skin

Amanda's Guide to Love

The Devil's Own Chloe

# Table of Contents

# Part I
# Proposition

# ONE

It is a truth universally acknowledged that a young man in possession of a vast fortune must be an entitled SOB born into money. Either that or a rags-to-riches a-hole who bulldozed his way to said fortune, leaving maimed bodies in his wake.

The ferocious-looking PA returns to her desk. "Monsieur Darcy is still in a meeting."

"That's OK." I smile benignly. "I can wait."

I place my hands demurely on my knees and stare at the portrait adorning—or should I say disfiguring—the wall across the hallway from where I'm seated.

Pictured is Count Sebastian d'Arcy du Grand-Thouars de Saint-Maurice, the oldest son of the late Count Thibaud d'Arcy du Grand-Thouars de Saint-Maurice and the inheritor of an estate estimated at around one billion euros. Said estate isn't your run-of-the-mill stock holdings or start-up fortune. Oh no. It's made up of possessions that were handed down—uninterrupted and snowballing—all the way from the Middle Ages.

Even Robespierre and his fellow revolutionaries didn't get their greedy little hands on the d'Arcy fortune.

*What are the odds?*

Upon his father's premature demise ten years ago, young Sebastian moved back into the town house in the heart of Le Marais and took the reins of the family's main business. A twenty-three-year-old greenhorn at the time, you'd expect him to make tons of bad decisions and sink the company or, at least, diminish its value.

But no such luck.

Instead, Sebastian Darcy took Parfums d'Arcy from number three to the number one European flavor and fragrance producer—a feat that neither his illustrious grandfather nor his star-crossed father had managed to accomplish.

According to my research, also about ten years ago, the new count chose to go by "Darcy," abandoning the apostrophe and the rest of his status-laden name. I'm sure he only did it to fool those *beneath* him—which includes most everyone in a country that guillotined its royals—into believing that he sees himself as their equal.

*The hell he does.*

Sebastian Darcy is a stinking-rich aristocrat with instincts of an unscrupulous business shark. This means he qualifies in both the SOB and the a-hole categories.

No, scratch that. He *slays* both categories.

And I hate him more than words can say.

The straitlaced man on the wall seems to smirk. I shudder, my nerves taut to the point of snapping. Will they kick me out if I spit at the photo? Of course they will. I steal a glance at the PA stationed between me and Darcy's office. She looks like a cross between a human and a pit bull. I'm sure she'd love to stick something other than paper between the jaws of her sturdy hole punch.

My hand, for example.

But I didn't come here to fight with Darcy's PA. I'll keep my saliva in my mouth, my eyes cast down, my butt perched on the edge of the designer chair, and my knees drawn together and folded to the side.

Like the meek little mouse I'm trying to pass for.

After waiting three weeks, I'm careful not to arouse any suspicion in Pitbull's mind so she won't cancel my appointment with Darcy.

*Eyes on the prize, Diane!* Don't forget you're here to declare war by spitting in Count Sebastian Darcy's face, rather than at his photographic representation.

I look at the photo again, arranged in perfect symmetry between the portraits of his grandfather, Bernard, who founded the company, and his father, Thibaud, who almost put the lid on it. I know this because I've done my homework.

During my week-long research, I dug up every piece of information the Internet had to offer about Sebastian Darcy and his family. I was hoping to find dirt, and I did. The only problem was it was already out in the open-  -common knowledge, yesterday's news.

And completely useless as leverage.

Pitbull looks up from her smartphone. "Monsieur Darcy is delayed. Do you mind waiting a little longer?"

"No problem." I smile politely. "I'm free this afternoon."

She arches an eyebrow as if having a free afternoon is something reprehensible.

How I wish I could stick out my tongue! But instead I widen my already unnaturally wide smile.

She frowns, clearly not buying it.

I turn away and stare at Darcy's likeness again. In addition to the now-stale scandal, my research has revealed that Darcy is close to his middle brother, Raphael, and also to a longtime friend—Laurent something or other. Our vulture-man even managed to have a serious girlfriend for most of last year. A food-chain heiress, she looked smashing at the various soirées, galas, and fundraisers where she was photographed on his arm. Darcy was rumored to be so into his rich beauty he was about to propose. But then she suddenly dumped him about six months ago.

*Clever girl.*

He has no right to be happy when Dad's life is in shambles.

I won't stop until I crush him, even if it means I go to jail—or to hell—for using black-hat tactics. It's not as if they'd let me into heaven, anyway. I've already broken the arms and legs on Darcy's voodoo doll.

There's no turning back after you do that sort of thing.

The next step is to let the world know who he really is and hurt him in a variety of ways, big and small. And then, just before delivering the deathblow, let him know he's paying for his sins.

That's why my first move is to show him my face and make sure he remembers it and associates it with *unpleasantness*. That way, when the shit hits the fan, he'll know which creditor is collecting her debt.

Pitbull breaks me out of my dream world. "Monsieur Darcy's meeting is running late."

"That's OK, I can—"

"No," she cuts me off. "There's no point in waiting anymore. As soon as the meeting is over, he'll head to the 9th arrondissement, where he's expected at a private reception."

I stand up.

She glances at my bare ring finger. "Mademoiselle, I can reschedule for Friday, December twelfth. It's two months away, but that's the only—"

"Thank you, but that won't be necessary," I say.

I know exactly which reception Sebastian Darcy is going to tonight.

# TWO

## *Three months later*

"It might snow tonight." Octave holds my coat while I wrap a scarf around my neck. "Will monsieur be taking his supper at home?"

As always, I wince at "monsieur," but I do my best not to show it.

Grandpapa Bernard hired Octave before I was born. Roughly Papa's age and a bear of a man, Octave has worked for my family for thirty-odd years, rising from valet to *majordome*. He's seen Raphael, Noah, and me in all kinds of embarrassing situations young boys tend to get themselves into. I've asked him a thousand times to call me Sebastian.

All in vain.

Octave Rossi claims his respect for my *old* family name, my *noble* title, and my position in society is too strong for him to drop the "monsieur."

So be it.

"Yes," I say. "But I'll come home late, so please tell Lynette to make something light. And don't stay up for me."

He nods. "*Oui*, monsieur."

Chances are he'll be up until I get home.

Since I moved back into the town house after Papa's passing, Octave has been helpful in a way no one, not even Maman—especially not Maman—has ever been. All the little things, from paying electricity bills and hiring help to undertaking necessary repairs and planning reception menus, are taken care of with remarkable efficiency.

When he offered to assist me with correspondence, I insisted on doubling his salary. My argument was that he'd be saving me the expense of a second PA for private matters.

He caved in only after I threatened to move out and sell the house.

I trust him more than anyone.

"Morning, Sebastian! To the office?" my chauffeur, Greg, asks.

He, at least, doesn't have a problem calling me by my first name.

"We'll make a detour," I say as I climb into the Toyota Prius. "I need to see someone first."

I give him the address, and he drives me to the Franprix on rue de la Chapelle in the 18th arrondissement. Greg parks the car, and I march into the supermarket, scanning the cashiers' counters lined parallel to the shop windows.

*There she is!*

Diane Petit smiles at a customer as she hands her a bag of groceries. She'll be finishing her shift in about ten minutes, according to the private eye I hired to locate and tail her. I'll talk to her then.

Right now, I pretend to study the selection of batteries and gift cards on display not far from her desk. What I'm really doing is furtively surveying the firebrand who smashed a cream cake in my face in front of a few dozen people last October. At the time, the only thing I registered about her through my surprise and anger was *foxy*.

I've had ample opportunity to pour over her pretty face and eye-pleasing shape in the numerous close-ups the PI has supplied over the past few weeks. I've studied Diane in all kinds of situations and circumstances—at work with her customers, hanging out with her friends, and roaming the streets with her camera, immortalizing everyday scenes of Parisian life. She's hot, all right, but there's also something endearing about her, something unsophisticated and very un-Parisian.

In spite of her extravagant outburst at Jeanne's bash, Diane Petit seems to be an unpretentious small-town bumpkin through and through.

I've learned a good deal about her since that memorable evening. I know she works part time at this supermarket, lives in a high-rise in the 14th, and hangs out with her foster sister Chloe, a coworker named Elorie, and a waitress named Manon.

She enjoys photographing random things, going to the movies, eating chocolate, and drinking cappuccino.

More importantly, I know why Diane did what she did that night at *La Bohème*.

And I plan to use it to my advantage.

Someone gives me a sharp prod in the back.

"Why are you here?" Diane asks as I spin around.

"To give you a chance to apologize."

She smirks. "You're wasting your time."

"No apology, then?"

"You're here to let me know you're on to me, right?" She puffs out her chest. "Read my lips—I'm not afraid of you."

"That's not why I'm here."

"How did you find me, anyway?"

"I hired a professional who tracked you down within days."

She tilts her head to the side. "And you've waited three months before confronting me. Why?"

"I wanted to know what your deal was, so I gave my PI the time to compile a solid profile." I hesitate before adding, "Besides, your foster sister was shot, and you were busy looking after her. I wanted to wait until Chloe had fully recovered."

"You've met Chloe?" She sounds surprised.

"Of course." I shrug. "Jeanne introduced us."

She blows out her cheeks. "What do you want, Darcy?"

"Just to talk."

"About what?"

"I have a proposition that might interest you."

She looks me over. "Unless your proposition is to give me a magic wand that would turn you into a piglet, I'm not interested."

"I obviously can't do that, but what I can do is—"

"Hey, Elorie, are we still on?" Diane calls to a fellow cashier who passes by.

Elorie smiles. "Only if you and Manon let me choose the movie."

"Fine with me, but I can't vouch for Manon."

While Diane and Elorie discuss the time and place of their outing, I resolve to draw Diane somewhere else before making my offer. Preferably, somewhere that's on my turf rather than hers.

"Can we go someplace quieter?" I ask Diane after Elorie leaves.

She sighs. "OK, but don't take it as a good sign."

"Understood."

I do take it as a step in the right direction, though.

She follows me outside and into the car.

"To Le Big Ben, please," I say to Greg.

He nods, and thirty minutes later, Diane and I are seated in a private booth at my favorite Parisian gentlemen's club, which I also happen to co-own with Raphael as of three weeks ago. We've kept the old manager, who's doing an admirable job. I've continued coming here with Laurent or Raph, as a longtime patron who enjoys the subdued elegance of this place and its unparalleled selection of whiskeys. The staff may not even realize the club has changed hands. It's easier this way—and it removes the need for socializing with them.

"So," Diane says after the server brings my espresso and her cappuccino. "What's your proposition?"

"Marry me."

She blinks and bursts out laughing as if I just said something outrageous. Which I guess it was without prior explanation.

Maybe I should start over.

"Here's the deal," I say. "You and I will *date* through April." I make air quotes when I say "date."

She looks at me as if I've lost my mind.

"You'll *move in* with me in May," I continue. "About a month after that, we'll get *married*."

Diane makes a circular motion with her index at the side of her head and mouths, "Nutcase."

"A month into our marriage, I'll *cheat* on you," I continue, undeterred, with a quote unquote on *cheat*. "And then you'll *leave* me."

She gives me a long stare. "Why?"

"It doesn't concern you. What you need to know is that I'm prepared to pay fifty thousand euros for a maximum of six months in a pretend relationship."

"Why?" she asks again.

"You don't need to know that."

"OK, let me ask you something I do need to know." She arches an eyebrow. "Why *me*?"

I shrug.

"If you continue ignoring my legitimate questions," she says, "I'm out of here before you finish your espresso."

"You're perfect for a plan I'd like to set in motion," I say. "And as an incentive for you to play your role the best you can, I'll quadruple your fee if my plan succeeds."

"How will I know if it succeeds if you won't even tell me what it is?"

"Trust me, you'll know." I smirk. "Everyone in my entourage will."

Diane leans back with her arms crossed over her chest. "Can't you find another candidate for your shady scheme? It couldn't have escaped your notice that I humiliated you in public."

"I assure you it didn't," I say. "But what's really important and valuable here is that it didn't escape other people's notice, either. A picture of my cream-cake-covered mug even ended up in a tabloid or two."

She gives me a smug smile.

"At the time, I told everyone I didn't know you, but I can easily change my tune and *confess* we'd been dating."

"This doesn't make any sense."

"Believe me, it does—a whole lot of sense—if you consider it in light of my scheme."

"Which I can't do," she cuts in, "because you won't tell me what your scheme is."

*True.* "Anyway, I'll tell everyone we've talked it over and made up."

She says nothing.

"Mademoiselle Petit... Diane." I lean in. "Your parents—and yourself—are *not* in the best financial shape right now. I'm offering an easy solution to your woes."

"Ha!" she interjects with an angry gleam in her almond-shaped eyes. "Says the person who caused our woes!"

She's right, of course, but not entirely. Before going in for the kill, I did offer to buy out her father's fragrance company. The offer wasn't generous by any measure, but it was reasonable given the circumstances. Charles Petit's artisanal workshop wasn't doing terribly well. In fact, it was of little interest to me, with the exception of the two or three of his signature fragrances that were worth the price I'd offered.

Charles is a lousy businessman—but he's a true artist. He *created* the fragrances he sold, and he also created for others. I would've offered him a job in one of my labs had I not been one hundred percent sure he'd decline it.

As it happened, he also declined my fifty thousand, calling me a scumbag and a few other choice epithets I won't repeat in front of a lady. Fifty thousand euros isn't a fortune, but seeing as he stood no chance against me, he should've taken the money.

It was better than nothing.

But Charles Petit proved to be more emotional than rational about his business. And he ended up with nothing. Worse than nothing, actually. I heard he took to drinking, got kicked out by his wife, and had a heart attack. Or was it a stroke?

Anyway, my point is, at least some of those misfortunes could've been avoided had he sold his company to me.

I open my mouth to say this to Diane, but then it occurs to me she must already know about my offer. She probably also shares Monsieur Petit's opinion that it was indecently low.

"Can we skip the whole dating and marrying nonsense," Diane says, "and go straight to the part where you grovel at my dad's feet, thrust a check for two hundred thousand into his hand, and beg him to take it in the hopes he might forgive you one day?"

I sigh and shake my head.

She stands. "The answer is no."

"Why don't you think it over? I'll be in touch next week." I set a twenty on the table. "May I offer you a ride?"

"Thank you, Monsieur Darcy, you're very *kind*." She bares her teeth in a smile that doesn't even try to pass for a real one. "But I prefer the *métro*."

# THREE

"Will you remind me again why we're on a *bus* just before the rush hour?" Elorie gives me a sour look, hugging her counterfeit Chanel bag to her chest.

I admit, it was a mistake. But I'm not admitting this out loud.

"It takes us straight to the bistro I've been telling you about," I say. "Like a taxi."

Elorie snorts. "Taxi, my foot! When I take a cab, I sprawl comfortably and give this baby"—she points at her bag—"its own seat. Whereas now—"

She jostles the woman on her left. "Madame, you're stepping on my foot!"

The woman apologizes and shifts a couple of inches, which is no mean feat, considering how packed the bus is.

Elorie turns back to me. "You said the bistro was in the 9th, yes?"

I nod.

"At this rate, it'll take us an hour to get there."

I'm about to suggest we get off and find the nearest *métro* station when two school kids jump out of their seats and make their way to the exit.

We take their seats immediately.

"Ah," Elorie says. "This is better. Not a taxi by a long shot, but still."

We're on this bus because I'm taking Elorie to celebrate at *La Bohème*, my favorite bistro in Paris. Perhaps even more than its amazing cappuccinos and out-of-this-world chocolate mousse, I love that bistro because it's home to two terrific chicks—Manon and Jeanne. Headwaiter Manon is my gym and movies companion, and she's the sweetest person I've ever met. Proprietor Jeanne's personality is so mood enhancing she should charge a supplement every time she tends the bar. Jeanne also happens to have a brother, Hugo, who happens to be my sister Chloe's fiancé. In other words, she's almost family.

*How cool is that?*

Regardless, I'd half expected her to declare me persona non grata for crashing her latest reception and assaulting one of her guests. The guest in question—Sebastian Darcy—is her husband's friend and political backer, which makes my smashing a cream cake in his face an even bigger affront. But Jeanne just laughed the incident off, saying the bash had been too stuffy and in serious need of an icebreaker.

Which I kindly provided.

The Manon-Jeanne combo makes me feel truly welcome at *La Bohème*. So much so that I forget I'm far away from home in a metropolis of eleven million people, suburbs included. The vast majority of them are crammed into tiny apartments and deeply convinced they're the most evolved representatives of the human race. Here in Paris, if you say *bonjour* to a stranger on the street, they think you're either a nutcase or a hooker.

"How's *the quest* coming along?" I ask Elorie.

*The quest* is shorthand for Elorie's newfound mission—locate an eligible billionaire and get him to marry her. Elorie defines "eligible" as currently available, reasonably young, and passably good-looking.

She launched the project three months ago on her twenty-sixth birthday, and she's been working hard on it ever since. Not very successfully, judging by the sound of it. But what's three months when looking for a soul mate who meets such high standards and such specific… specifications?

"I've made good progress," Elorie says.

I bug out my eyes. "I want a name!"

"Not so fast, *ma cocotte*. My progress is theoretical at this point."

"Oh."

"Don't you *oh* me." Elorie wags her index finger from side to side. "Would you launch a business without conducting a market study first?"

"I guess not." I narrow my eyes. "Do you approach all your dreams as a business?"

She shrugs. "Not all—only the ones worth pursuing. Anyway, as the saying goes, if you practice without theory, you shall fall into the ditch."

"There's no such saying."

"You sure?" She puts her chin up. "Well, there should be. Anyway, I stand on much firmer ground today than three months ago all because I've done enough research to write a thesis on the topic."

"Maybe you should write one," I mutter.

Elorie is the most entertaining person I've ever met and I love her, but her pragmatism does rattle me sometimes. Then again, I'm well aware I'm a country-fried prawn who still hasn't wrapped her head around big-city attitudes.

"Ha-ha, very funny!" Elorie pauses before adding, "Anyway, I've now read all the tutorials and how-to articles I could get my hands on, and I've analyzed several real-life case studies."

"I'm impressed."

"Me, too," she says with a wink. "I've never taken anything so seriously in my whole life."

"*Mesdames, messieurs,*" the bus driver says into the speaker. "This bus will not continue beyond Opéra. You can wait for the next one or take an alternate route."

People gripe and boo and begin to move toward the doors.

I spread my arms in apology.

Elorie rolls her eyes.

We get off and continue our journey using the most reliable means of transportation in Paris—our feet. The air is cold and humid, which is no surprise in February, but at least it isn't raining.

I look up at the leaden sky and tone down my gratitude—it isn't raining *yet*.

"Feel like sharing your theoretical findings?" I ask, tucking my scarf inside my coat in an attempt to shield myself from the cutting wind.

Elorie considers my request. "OK. But only because you're my friend and you always pay for the drinks."

"Aww." I place my hand on my heart. "You put 'friend' before 'drinks,' you wonderful person."

"Listen up—because I won't repeat this," Elorie says, choosing to ignore my irony. "The single most important action you can take is to hang out where billionaires do."

"In Swiss banks?"

"For example." She nods, unfazed. "Don't tell me you believe Kate would've snatched William if her clever mom hadn't sent her to the University of St Andrews, where the cream of British nobility goes?"

"I must confess I haven't given the matter much thought."

"Then thank me for opening your eyes."

"Thank you," I say dutifully. "But we have a problem—I'm too old for college, and it isn't my thing, anyway."

"That's OK," she says. "It was just an example."

"Phew." I'm doing my best to keep my expression earnest. "What a load off!"

She glances at me sideways and shakes her head. "What I'm telling you isn't funny, Diane. It's precious. I'd be taking notes if I were you."

"Sorry, sweetie. Go on."

"I'll give you a few pointers," she says. "Go horseback riding, join a golf club, or book yourself into a high-end ski resort. If you're targeting a specific man, go exactly where he goes."

"Some people would call it stalking."

"*I* call it lending fate a hand."

"OK," I say. "What about the rich perverts who frequent BDSM clubs? Should I get a membership for one? And what about the polygamists who make their wives wear burkas? Where do you draw the line?"

"Where he buys me Louboutin pumps, Prada sunglasses, and Chanel purses to wear with my burka." She arches an eyebrow. "If I can travel the world in his private jet and have my own wing in his palace plus three or four maids at my beck and call, then sure, why not. Bring on the burka."

I stop and put my hands on my hips.

Elorie stops, too.

"Aren't you a little too cavalier about this?" My voice betrays my feelings—equal parts incredulity and concern. "Let me be more specific. We're not talking a *burkini* here. We're talking the works with gloves and an eye grid. And *other* wives."

Elorie tilts her head to the side, thinking. "Ten maids, my own palace, and my own jet."

I'm too dumbfounded to speak.

"What?" she says. "Don't look at me like that. Everyone has a price, and so do you."

"I don't think so."

"Of course, you do. You're just too ashamed to admit it, which is kind of sad."

Does she really think that?

"Or maybe you're fooling yourself that your affections can't be bought," she says, her expression pensive. "Which is even sadder."

"Please, believe me when I say I don't care about money." I stare her in the eye. "I don't mind having some—just enough to get by—but I wouldn't make the slightest sacrifice just so I can marry a rich man."

Elorie rolls her eyes, clearly not buying it.

"If you want to know the truth," I say, "I find rich men repulsive. They're so full of themselves, so convinced of their superiority! They gross me out."

"What, all of them?" she asks, raising an eyebrow.

"Without exception. They mistake their dumb luck for divine providence and their lack of scruples for business acumen."

Elorie narrows her eyes. "It sounds like you're talking about one rich man in particular. And I think it's Sebastian Darcy."

The moment she mentions his name, I realize I've spent the past few weeks doing exactly what Elorie just advised me to do—researching a rich man. But there's a difference. I haven't been investigating him for a chance to marry him. I've been probing into his life in the hopes of finding a weapon to destroy him.

I didn't find any.

And then, three days ago, he showed up at my workplace and handed me one.

Sure, what he's offered is a stick rather than a hatchet. But it's up to me to take that stick and sharpen it into a spear. Our ancestors killed mammoths with spears—I should be able to skewer a man.

"He's superhot, by the way," Elorie says. "I'd marry him even if he was a mere millionaire."

"He's a jerk."

"Who isn't?"

I start walking again. "So you meet the billionaire of your dreams, then what?"

"Duh." She rolls her eyes. "Then I make him fall madly in love with me."

"Of course! How?"

"By being gorgeous, self-confident, and classy."

I clear my throat audibly.

"What was that supposed to mean?" she asks, turning to me.

"We're cashiers." I give her a hard stare. "We may be called *cute* but *gorgeous* and *classy* *are* beyond our reach."

I expect her to object that you can be classy on a budget, but instead she puts her arm around my shoulders and gives a gentle squeeze.

"Finally," she says with an approving smile. "Diane Petit has demonstrated there's a realist hiding in there, underneath her *principles* and other bullshit."

Her words sting a little.

"My dear," Elorie says as we turn onto rue Cadet. "I'll reward your bout of honesty by giving you the single most precious piece of advice anyone has ever given you. Or ever will."

I halt again and fold my hands across my chest. "I'm all ears."

"I'm sharing this," Elorie says, "because we're besties and because I want you to owe me one."

I shake my head. "You can't link those two reasons with an *and*. They're mutually exclusive. It's either because we're besties *or* because you want me to owe you one."

She sucks on her teeth for a brief moment. "I want you to owe me one."

"OK, what's your precious advice?"

"It's a shortcut that very few women are aware of."

"Yeees?"

"You need to develop a real interest and a certain level of competence in what the billionaires you're targeting are passionate about."

I pull a face. "Things like football?"

"If that's what floats his boat."

"I see."

"It can be all sorts of things." Elorie begins to count on her fingers. "Sports cars. War movies. Guns. High tech gadgets. Video games."

"I think they're a waste of time," I say.

"It doesn't matter what you think. What matters is what you say." She moves on to her right hand. "Mixed martial arts. Wine. Politics. Porn. Art photography."

My eyebrows shoot up.

She giggles. "That last one was a mole to check if you were paying attention. Nobody—except you, that is—cares about art photography."

"I know men who do."

"Are they filthy rich?"

I shake my head.

"Ha! Thought so."

We reach *La Bohème*, and I stop in front of the entrance, pulling Elorie by her sleeve to stop her from walking on.

"OK," I say. "Let's finish this conversation before we go in. Let's say you've become a wine connoisseur or a sports car buff. How does that guarantee your billionaire will fall to your feet like an electrocuted wasp?"

"It's science, dum-dum." She cocks her head. "Say your man loves Star Wars and football. You give him a well-timed Yoda quote, and his mind goes, 'Ooh, she's special.' Then you give him an analysis of the latest Paris Saint-Germain victory, and his body releases even more happiness hormones. And before he knows it, his brain learns to associate that euphoric state with you. This leads him to conclude you're Mademoiselle Right, which, in turn, leads him to propose."

"Neat," I say.

And what about the billionaire who proposes not because he gives a shit if you're Mademoiselle Right or Mademoiselle One Night, but because he wants to use you in some shady scheme?

I push open the door to the bistro and decide to keep that last observation to myself.

# FOUR

"So what are we celebrating?" Elorie asks after we settle at the bar and Manon hands us two tall glasses of *vin chaud*.

The steaming mulled wine smells of cinnamon and orange. It makes my frozen insides relax with comfort and my brain thaw with a pleasant mist in a way that's satisfying beyond words.

Who needs orgasms when you can just take a walk out in the cold and drink this ambrosia?

I grab the spoon in my glass and pull out the half slice of orange begging to be eaten. "Have you heard of *Voilà Paris*?"

"The gossip magazine?"

"They call themselves a women's magazine, but yes, gossip is their main stock in trade." I bite into my orange slice. "They bought some of my pics last month, and now they're hiring me on as a freelance photojournalist."

Elorie frowns. "You're going to be a paparazzo."

I shake my head, unable to speak because of the wine in my mouth.

"They publish articles, too, not just celebrity gossip," Manon says.

I swallow the wine. "The deal is if I produce fun pictures with original captions, they'll let me put them together into a story."

"Congratulations, Diane!" Manon high-fives me and jogs away to take care of other customers.

"Yeah, congrats," Elorie says with a lot less enthusiasm. "Does this mean you'll resign from the supermarket?"

"I can't. Freelancing pays for movie tickets and drinks, but there's also the little matter of rent."

Elorie nods, perking up.

We hang out at *La Bohème* for another hour and then head home. Elorie catches an RER train to her parents' suburban cottage, and I take the *métro* to Chloe's apartment in the 14th. In fact, I should stop thinking of it as Chloe's. Now that she's moved in with Hugo and I've taken over the lease, the place is officially mine.

The next morning, I wake up with a headache that's too strong for the two glasses of mulled wine I had last night. Then I remember I hardly slept, weighing the pros and cons with regards to Darcy's offer just as I'd done the night before and the night before that.

I pop an aspirin and head to the shower.

Darcy's proposition has been on my mind nonstop for three days now. No matter how I turn it, taking him up on his offer is a no-brainer. Basically, there are only two ways this can go. Option A, I play his game and pocket the funds for Dad. Option B, I pretend to play his game, but in reality, I seize the opportunity to poke around his house and dig up some dirt on him. Once I have the info and the evidence, I'll get it published in *Voilà Paris* or leak it to a more serious periodical, depending on the nature of the scoop. This will, hopefully, do some serious damage to Darcy's finances or, at least, tarnish his reputation.

Maybe both. And thus avenge Dad.

My brain prefers Option A, while my gut craves Option B. But here's the best part—I win, no matter how the dice roll, and Dad gets either money or satisfaction. Or both, if I can find dirt and be patient enough to hold onto it until after I am paid. That would make me a villain, and a nasty piece of work, but who says being ruthless is men's prerogative?

Sebastian Darcy is a vulture. He deserves a taste of his own cruelty.

It's in that crucial instant, right after I've shampooed my hair and just before I rinse it, that I decide I'll marry him.

* * *

We meet in his office because Darcy's schedule for today has only one thirty-minute slot that could be freed.

"I'm glad you were able to see that my offer represents a unique opportunity for you and your family," he says, motioning me to the *informal* area of his ginormous office with comfy leather armchairs and a designer coffee table.

His arrogance is unbearable, but I hold my tongue. If I want my plan to succeed, I need him to trust me.

Pitbull enters with a tray loaded with drinks, pretty little sandwiches, and mouthwatering pastries. She gives me a perplexed look, which tells me she remembers me from my cancelled appointment back in October and wonders if she's pegged me right.

"Could you maybe clue me in on the whys of your offer?" Rather than sitting down, I go to the floor-to-ceiling window and take in the breathtaking view. "It would help to know what I'm getting myself into."

"I explained last time," he says. "And I can assure you it's not illegal or dangerous."

I turn around and give him a stare. "You didn't explain anything. You just said 'I need you to be my pretend girlfriend for a couple of months and then my pretend wife for another month or so.' "

"And that's as much as you need to know," he says, his voice dry. "Take it or leave it."

*Fine. Don't tell me. I'll find out on my own.*

"Will you please sit down?" He points to the sofa. "I'd like you to look at the contract."

*Ah, so there's a written contract. Well, what did I expect?*

I amble over to one of the armchairs, plonk myself down, and pick up an éclair. "I'm not going to sign your contract right away."

"I don't expect you to." He sits down opposite me. "You can study it tonight and call me tomorrow morning, but you can't discuss it with anyone. That's why you'll need to sign *this* before you can see the contract."

He nudges a sheet of paper across the coffee table. The title at the top of the page says, "Nondisclosure Agreement."

How clever of him.

I read and sign the agreement while Darcy wolfs down a few sandwiches, explaining he hasn't had time to eat yet.

Who knew billionaires were such busy people?

"We'll use your dramatic appearance at Jeanne and Mat's party to our best advantage," he says, wiping his fingers with a napkin.

"How?"

"I'll tell everyone we'd been seeing each other discreetly for a few months until you were led to believe I'd cheated on you. But now the misunderstanding is cleared up and we're back together, madly in love."

I narrow my eyes. "Why go out of your way to give a reason for what I did when you can just fall *madly in love* with a fresh face who won't require any explaining."

"Because what you did suggests you're the kind of woman who doesn't put up with cheating."

"And that's good becaaaause...?"

"I can't tell you, but trust me, it's good. In fact, it's perfect for my plan."

I sigh. "Whatever you say."

"Let's look at the contract now, shall we?" He glances at his watch. "My meeting starts in fifteen minutes."

I open the manila folder and stare at the document inside it.

"Most of it is legalese that we can go over next time once we agree on the terms," Darcy says.

I nod.

"You can go straight to this part." He turns several pages and points at a paragraph with bullet points. "Please read this and let me know if you have questions. Or, if you prefer, I can just walk you through it."

I scoff at him. "Coming from a family that's been sending its children to private schools for generations, you may not be aware that France has had free universal education since the 1880s."

He blinks, clearly taken aback. "I'm sorry. I didn't mean to offend you."

"No, it's me who's sorry to shatter your aristocratic illusions," I say. "But cashiers can read."

"I was just trying to be helpful," he says.

I know he is. And it aggravates me. I'd be much more comfortable with him if he'd stop hiding his ugly face behind this mask of polite concern.

Darcy looks at his watch again and taps his index finger on the highlighted passage. "Read this at home, then reread it, and write down all your questions. I'll call you tomorrow night."

Aha, now he's showing his bossy side.

I'm so intimidated.

*Not*.

"*Oui*, monsieur." I bow my head with exaggerated obedience, noting in passing that Darcy has handsome hands—lean wrists, large palms, and long fingers.

At least the right one, which is currently pinning the contract to the table.

Let's hope his left hand is teeny-weeny. Or super fat. Or excessively hairy.

He doesn't deserve two handsome hands.

"The gist of this paragraph," Darcy says, "is that you recognize you're entering a financially compensated transaction with me, which is couched as a relationship, but is *not* a relationship, be it physical or emotional."

A relationship with an a-hole.

*God forbid.*

"Consider it recognized," I say.

"It also says here somewhere…" He slides his finger along the lines and halts on one of the bullet points. "Here—it says you commit to moving in with me at about the two-month mark on our timeline."

"Do I have to?"

"This has to be credible for it to work." He makes a sweeping gesture with his other hand, which, unfortunately, is as nicely shaped as the first. "A month after that, I'll propose, and another month after that, we'll marry."

"It'll look rushed. Besides, how are you going to stage a town hall ceremony and—"

"I won't have to. We'll fly to the Bahamas for a week and get *married* there." He uses air quotes.

"Wow, you've thought this through."

"I have, indeed." He clears his throat. "As you can see, the bullet point just below states that sex is not a requirement but you *will* need to touch and kiss me in public."

"Good."

He raises his eyebrows in surprise.

*Crap.* That came out all wrong.

"What I meant was it's good that sex isn't required. It would've been a deal-breaker."

He nods. "That's what I thought."

"Do I *have* to kiss you?"

"Yes. It doesn't have to be torrid. But if we never kiss, our relationship won't look convincing."

"OK, if we must." I sigh. "So we date, move in together, and smooch on camera. Then what?"

"Then we wait for… a certain person to make his move."

"How very enigmatic." I roll my eyes. "You do realize I'm going to hate every moment of our time together, right?"

"You won't be the only one," he says. "In any event, if nothing happens within six months, we'll break up and I'll pay you for your time. But if my plan works, you'll walk away a rich woman."

Or if *my* plan works, you'll be left a ruined man.

# Part II
# Island

# FIVE

"Did Belle Auxbois at least say she'd think about it?"

I turn to glance at Dad, who's slumped in the passenger seat, fuming. I take it the pop star made no such promise. It doesn't surprise me. The diva demonstrates typical rich-person behavior—exploit whomever you can, whenever you can, for as long as you can. Come to think of it, this credo must be the most important qualification for joining the Rich Club.

The only real difference between Belle Auxbois and Darcy is that her fake sweetness and angelic voice have misled millions of people into thinking she's a nice person.

Dad and I are in his car, and I'm driving him home from his physical therapy session. The poor man hates these sessions with all his heart. I don't blame him. His therapist is a hulk of a woman with sadistic propensities. She would've made a formidable Grand Inquisitor in another time and place, wringing confessions of witchcraft and heresy from innocent souls. But luckily for the medievals and unluckily for us, Troll Queen isn't an officer of the Inquisition. She's employed by a public hospital just outside of Marseille.

It took me six weekends with Dad and trips to the hospital's rehab center to figure out her deal. This meant hours of watching her walk and talk—in fact, "bark" would be a better word for her unique communication style—and listening to grown men and women begging for mercy behind her door.

Have you ever tried to read a book while your beloved daddy screams, "Please, I can't take it anymore!" next door?

I have.

And I didn't enjoy it.

Anyway, Mamma Grizzly is convinced that stroke rehab protocol has to be painful to be effective. And God forbid someone confuses what she does for a living with massage. Because, you see, madame isn't a masseuse. Hell, no. Her job is *not* to rub and knead people into comfort. Her job is to twist and contort patients into recovery.

To be fair, Dad *has* improved dramatically since the dominatrix first laid her hands on him. He can now move his fingers and speak more distinctively.

And that's the only reason I haven't sued her. Instead, I always make sure my smartphone is fully charged before we head to the hospital. When we get there, I stick my earplugs in my ears and let System of a Down outshout Dad.

"What exactly did Belle say when you called her?" I ask again.

He turns to me. "It's a no-go. She cited the contract."

That damn contract! Why hadn't he shown it to me before signing?

"Did you try to appeal to her humanity? Explain how much it would mean to you in your current situation?"

"Yeah, I did." He sighs and turns away to stare at the road. "She said she was sorry, but she couldn't do it."

"Not even to admit you gave her a hand? Or that she consulted you?"

"You see,"—he lets out a bitter snort—"Madame Auxbois was featured on some morning show a couple of days ago, where she told the *whole country* she'd concocted the perfume in her kitchen. All by herself."

I blow my cheeks out. "That's ridiculous."

*Stupid cow!*

I glance at Dad's defeated face, and my heart aches with pity. If I want to help him—and God knows I do more than anything in the world—I must get better at channeling my anger into something constructive.

Count your blessings, Diane.

For one, Dad's arm is on the mend, and his speech has improved so much it's hard to imagine I had trouble understanding him a year ago. He's joined AA and hasn't had a drop of alcohol since his stroke.

And last but not least, I'm about to get an unhoped-for chance to hurt his archenemy—Sebastian Darcy.

We met briefly yesterday to sign the contract and iron out the details. I tried all the powers of persuasion I'm capable of to waive the requirement of living under his roof. But he was firm. He said his immediate circle had to believe we were consumed by mad passion. It was crucial to the success of his scheme. I'm deducing—clever me—that his scheme targets someone in his entourage.

I also tried to persuade him to let Chloe and Elorie in on our charade. Chloe is family and Elorie is my best friend in Paris. They know me well, especially Chloe. It would be hard to lie to them.

The answer was no way. The only person in the loop besides the two of us is his brother Raphael, but only because they hatched the plan together. Aside from that exception, no one else must know. Every additional person who has the info increases the risk of a leak and, consequently, the failure of his plan. With an icy gleam in his eyes, he reminded me I had committed to secrecy by signing the nondisclosure agreement and he had every intention of holding me to it.

*You do that, genius.*

Whoever drafted that agreement—I suspect it was Darcy and his bro all by themselves, seeing his obsession with confidentiality—left a loophole. The text focuses too much on the fake relationship and things around it. But there's nothing in it that says I must keep my lips sealed with regards to unrelated trivial secrets I might stumble upon, such as tax evasion or financial fraud.

Or less trivial ones, such as murder.

I almost drooled as I pictured myself finding proof that the senior Darcy's death wasn't accidental. Lo and behold, he was killed in cold blood by his oldest son, Sebastian. The golden boy will be investigated, found guilty, and sent to prison where he'll rot for rest of his days.

*Wouldn't that be a hoot?*

"Any other questions?" Darcy asked, breaking me out of my favorite fantasy.

I'd told him my biggest concern was how Dad would handle the news of our *association* once it reached his ears.

"He'll get over it," Darcy said, all dry pragmatism.

"He'll stop talking to me." I wrung my hands. "He'll think I'm a traitor."

"If it's any consolation, my mother thinks I'm a traitor."

Does she now? Is that why Marguerite d'Arcy has been holed up in Nepal doing charity work for over a decade? *Voilà Paris* called her "the French Mother Teresa" in the feature they ran about her a couple of years ago.

"Why would she think that?" I asked.

He sighed and waved my question off. "Long story."

I made a mental note to investigate.

Before we said good-bye, Darcy informed me that our first "post-reconcilliation" outing will be a "small, informal gathering" to celebrate his brother Raphael's twenty-ninth birthday. I pointed out I didn't know anyone in his circle. He said he'd invited Jeanne and Mat. Mat is an up-and-coming politician he believes in and backs. I'm friends with Jeanne. We can spend most of the weekend chatting with the couple. That way, neither of us will appear stiff to anyone watching.

I nodded, dropping my head so he wouldn't see me roll my eyes.

*Because, honestly, who are you kidding, man?*

You never smile. I've never seen you slump or stoop, be it in photos or in real life. Regardless of what you say or do, your body language, accent and manners scream, "Stuck-up aristocrat."

You don't just appear stiff—you're Count Stiff. No, you're King Stiff.

Brace yourself, your Majesty.

I'm here to depose you.

# SIX

I sip my iced tea and stare out the bay window at the waters of the Mediterranean. I'm no longer in Dad's cheap divorcé pad deep inside the ugliest industrial suburb of Marseille. This place is lush and unspoiled by construction folly. In fact, the only construction here is an unobtrusive energy-efficient villa overlooking the beach.

The "small, informal gathering" Darcy had told me about turned out to be a weekend party for over fifty guests. Held on a Greek island.

A *private* Greek island.

The guests were flown to Crete this morning by *private* jet—of course—all white leather and overwhelming sleekness. While up in the air, I met Darcy's middle brother, Raphael—the CEO of a large audit firm—his best friend, Laurent, and a bunch of other people, all of whom eyed me with unrestrained curiosity.

After we landed, I was eager to see the sites, but it looked as if I was the only one who'd never been to Crete before. Even Jeanne, the only other "normal" person in this jet set, had visited it when she backpacked around Europe at twenty.

"Another time," Darcy had said to me, all bossy and curt, before we were all ferried to Ninossos, farther south, on board a *private* mahogany-paneled yacht.

How else was a poor rich man to transport guests to his island?

"Papa loved this place," Darcy says, planting himself next to me. "The weather is mild here almost all year round."

I can definitely believe that, considering how sunny and warm it is right now in the middle of winter. The island is small and kept in its natural state, except for this villa. Perched on a hillside and separated from the sandy beach by terraced gardens, it offers a breathtaking view over the sea.

*What's not to love?*

"It's Raphael's now," Darcy says.

I give him a sidelong glance and turn away quickly, embarrassed by the effect his jeans and shirt are having on me. *Dammit!* When he wears one of his bespoke suits, I can tell myself it's not him, it's the cut. The second I catch myself eyeing his torso, I bring up the image of a Savile Row tailor wielding his magic scissors and turning amorphous men into hunks.

The problem is no sane person with functioning eyes would call the man standing next to me amorphous.

I force a sneer. "Is the boat his, too?"

He nods.

"And the jet?"

"We co-own it, the same as Le Big Ben."

"I hadn't pegged you as someone who's into *sharing*, even with family members."

"You're wrong—I do share, and not only with family. My other jet is used for corporate travel by all Parfums d'Arcy managers and sales reps."

I shake my head, tut-tutting. "How disappointing. Billionaires aren't what they used to be."

He says nothing.

I sneak a peek at him. Darcy's expression is as stony as ever. It's not as if I expected him to crack up or anything, but… I don't know… maybe smile a little?

*Forget it.*

Who cares what he thinks, anyway?

I point at the picture-perfect young people who sunbathe and entertain themselves in a variety of beachy ways a couple dozen meters from the villa. "I'll go find Jeanne."

"Of course," he says. "I'll go chat with the caterer and the local staff and make sure everything's ready for the party tonight."

I scrunch my eyebrows. "Shouldn't Raphael do that? It's *his* birthday."

"Raphael should relax and enjoy himself," Darcy says. "It's his *birthday*."

Righto.

With a canned smile, I hand him my empty glass and head outside.

The first thing that jumps out at me as the soles of my feet touch the sand is just *how much* Raphael is enjoying himself. Reclining on his back, the birthday boy is letting a topless Scarlett Johansson doppelgänger on his left smear sunscreen onto his tanned chest. While she's at it, a topless clone of Natalie Portman on his right giggles at something he said.

*Seriously?*

I look around. Am I the only one who finds this utterly ridiculous?

Oh, wait! Maybe the trio is reenacting *The Other Boleyn Girl.*

Yes, that must be it.

I avert my gaze, scanning the beach crowd for Jeanne.

Honestly, what did I expect? Rich men are all like that—spoiled and obnoxious. I'm sure Raphael's older brother engages in similar pursuits when he isn't in a fake relationship with a girl who shudders at the thought of kissing him. To say nothing of engaging in a threesome with him. My antipathy to Darcy aside, I'd have to be unconscious or dead to be involved in a threesome with anyone—even a man I lusted after.

If I ever met such a man.

"Hey, Diane!" Raphael waves enthusiastically while "Scarlett" and "Natalie" peer at me, giving off distinctly hostile vibes. "Over here!"

Er... *I don't think so.* "I'm looking for Jeanne."

"Mat's wife? I saw them inside." He stands up and saunters toward me in all his bare-chested glory.

I wonder if his brother's muscles are as well defined as his. Then I wonder why I'm wondering this.

"You should ask Seb to give you a tour of the island," he says, looking me over.

I give him a pointed *cut-the-crap* look.

He shrugs with a hint of defiance, as if to say, *I'm just playing my part and so should you.*

Oh, well, I guess I should. There are doppelgängers within earshot, after all. And, judging by how quiet they've suddenly grown, they're all ears.

"Great idea." I force a smile. "Do you come here often?"

"Whenever I can. This is my favorite place on Earth."

"What's the deal with the *third* Darcy brother?" I ask. "He wasn't on the plane, was he?"

Raphael shakes his head, his grin fading a little.

"I haven't had the pleasure of meeting him yet," I say.

It's clear he doesn't relish the turn our small talk is taking, but I can't help myself. "Will he be arriving later, on a *regular* flight with all those poor millionaires crammed in business class?"

"Noah isn't coming," Raphael says, his smile strained now. "He had some... important business to take care of."

Birthday boy takes a sudden interest in his feet, as if he just discovered he had toes. It doesn't look as if he'll say more on the subject.

Never mind. None of the Darcy secrets will resist Diane Petit's power of observation.

*You just wait.*

"Raphael, come back here," Scarlett Johansson calls out, pouting. "You promised to return the sunscreen favor."

Natalie Portman mirrors her pout. "And I'm still waiting for my foot massage."

Raphael looks at me, obviously relieved. "I'd love to chat more, but I have promises to keep."

"Off you go," I say.

Behind me, someone jogs toward us. Before I have time to turn around, that someone puts his arm around my shoulders.

"Let me show you around this rock." Darcy says, pressing a kiss to my forehead. "Come, *chérie*."

I knit my brows. "Didn't your governess teach you that sneaking up on people is bad manners, *chéri*?"

A smile crinkles Raphael's eyes as he turns toward Darcy. "Is everything under control? Food delivered and servers lined up?"

Darcy hesitates. "If you really want to know, there was a small issue with the swimming pool. The caretaker couldn't get the new heating system to start."

"It's no big deal," Raphael says.

"You invited people to a poolside party, didn't you?" Darcy's tone is so distinctly older brotherly it reminds me of Lionel. "You don't want to let them down."

"You're right," Raphael says before turning to me. "We should all thank whatever deity we believe in for people like Seb. They make the world a better place."

*Yeah, sure.*

"Speaking of a better place." Raphael wrinkles his nose at Darcy. "Did you actually manage to fix the pool heater?"

"I managed to find the user manual," Darcy says. "And Kostas fixed the heating system."

Raphael taps his brother's shoulder. "I'll leave you to your girlfriend."

"Come." Darcy pulls my hand. "I want you to meet Laurent and some other friends."

I give him a canned smile. "I can't wait!"

What I really can't wait for is to go back home and barf.

# SEVEN

It's ten in the evening and the party is in full swing.

Darcy and I stand between two ancient olive trees, in a small circle of dressed people, most of whom are friends of Darcy's. The majority of his brother's crowd are in swimsuits and flock around the pool and the DJ, who's converted one of the decks into a dance floor.

I would've liked to plunge into the pool, too, and maybe dance a little. I'm closer both in age and attitude to the boisterous "Raphaelites" than the stuck-up "Sebastianers." But what I want to do is irrelevant. I'm here for work—not pleasure. That's what I tell myself every time Darcy wraps his arm around my shoulder or sets his hand on the small of my back to show his friends how much "in love" he is.

*Does he think they're stupid?*

I don't know about men, but I'm almost sure the women have us figured out by now. Our embraces are devoid of tenderness. The looks we exchange are cold, and the endearments we say to each other sound painfully fake.

But it's Darcy's problem, not mine. My contract says nothing about "good acting." As far as I'm concerned, all's well.

The DJ starts a new disk. It's by an unfamiliar artist, but one I'll certainly be looking up. The beat is so hard to resist that all of Raphael's standing and sitting friends begin to groove. One by one, the swimming ones come out of the pool, too, and join in the fun. The two Boleyn girls rock their nimble frames suggestively, no doubt to please their "king."

*Where is the birthday boy, by the way?*

I turn my head toward the barbecue grill. There he is, cooking batches of seafood, meat, and vegetables. Said batches—cleaned and skewered for him—are being ferried from the kitchen and, once off the grill, served by the catering staff.

I look away, trying not to sneer at this rich man's version of *hands-on* work.

A splash draws my attention to the pool where a vision in female form emerges. She makes me think of Botticelli's *Venus*. Minus the supersized shell. Plus a red bikini.

No part of her is beautiful, strictly speaking. But there's such confidence in her posture and in the way she surveys the crowd that you can't help wondering: *Am I missing something?* Could she be a royal princess from one of those napkin-sized countries around the Mediterranean? I try to run a facial recognition search in my mind, pulling up all the princesses I'd seen in gossip magazines when I'd done my "research."

No one matches Venus. Maybe she isn't royalty, after all, but simply the first woman I've met whose self-esteem feeds on something other than her looks. Could be money, wit, professional aptitude, unequalled skill or expertise in some area... Whatever it is, she has tons of it.

All around, heads turn and conversations falter.

Venus steps onto the deck and wrings her mane of silky hair, her gesture full of easy elegance.

Darcy follows my gaze. "Genevieve Lougnon, heiress to the Lougnon Champagne house. She's Raph's best friend since childhood."

Laurent gives me a wink. "My jaw dropped, too, when I saw Genevieve for the first time. But don't worry—you'll get used to her aplomb. Eventually."

Laurent is a surgeon and as middle-class as it gets in Darcy's inner circle.

Jeanne and Mat join our small group.

"You know," Mat says to Darcy. "I almost declined your invitation."

Darcy raises an eyebrow in surprise.

"It's one thing to have you back the Greens' European Parliament bid—for which I'm eternally grateful," Mat says. "But it's another to let you jet me to a poolside party on your private island."

"It's Raph's," Darcy says, ever the nitpicker. "I thought the Greens were outside the rich-poor divide."

"No political party really is, regardless of what they claim." Mat shrugs. "But it would, indeed, have been worse if I was a socialist."

"You think this could backfire?"

Mat gives him a wink. "If hard pressed, I'll say I only agreed to come here so I could study your top-notch low-energy house."

"You know what's funny?" Jeanne says to Darcy. "Mat actually did spend three hours this afternoon crawling all over the house and taking notes."

"Unfortunately,"—Darcy smiles—"nobody will believe him."

It's the first time I've seen him smile. His face lights up and transforms in a most unexpected way. There's mirth in his eyes. His lips, usually pressed together in a hard line, part and show white teeth. His body relaxes, and the permanent stick up his posterior seems to dissolve as if by magic. He looks almost... charming.

"Unfair but true," Mat says.

Jeanne gives her husband an affectionate look— the kind neither Darcy nor I can ever produce for each other, even if our lives depended on it.

"Hey, hon." Jeanne turns to me. "I heard from Chloe about your dad's struggle to get credited for his new perfume. What a bummer."

I shrug. "Belle Auxbois said she'd sue him if she saw his name mentioned anywhere in relation to it."

"So it's in the contract?" Mat asks. "Wasn't he aware of her terms when he signed it?"

I sigh. "It's not that simple. The contract says she may 'wish to but doesn't have to' credit Dad. It's written in fine print, tucked away on one of the last pages. When he read it before signing, he saw what he wanted to see."

"Poor Charles." Jeanne gives my arm a squeeze. "He assumed she'd recognize his 'help' like the other celebs he's worked with in the past, right?"

I nod.

"The road to hell is paved with assumptions," Darcy says.

Neither his tone nor his expression betrays an ounce of the sympathy that Jeanne and Mat's comments conveyed.

*Self-righteous ass.*

He does have a point, of course. I've lost count of how many times Mom and I have told Dad he needs to quit being such an idealist and learn to plan for contingencies. We've also begged him to expect his clients and business partners to try to screw him over.

Because most of them will, given the chance.

So, yeah, I do agree with the point he's making, but my agreement doesn't make his remark more palatable. I guess it's the way he delivered it—injecting it with such superiority—that turned my stomach.

He must think he's so much better than Dad! Than all of us lowborn provincials. Bile rises in my throat. I know I should let this slide, but the itch to bite back is stronger than me. Must have something to do with family honor, I suspect.

The Darcys versus the Petits.

I pick up a seafood platter and hold it up for my *boyfriend*. "Let he who is without assumption cast the first prawn at me."

He stares into my eyes, saying nothing.

I shrug and put the platter down. "I'm not feeling well. Must be the oysters or just a stomach bug."

"I can give you some of my SMECTA," Jeanne says quickly. "I never travel without it!"

"It's OK—I'll be fine tomorrow morning. What I need is sleep." I wave my hand. "Night-night, everyone."

The group wishes me a good night, and I withdraw into the house.

Did I mention I'm sharing a bedroom with Darcy?

Thankfully, it's huge and has a nice big couch in addition to the king-size bed. Darcy kindly offered to sleep on the couch. I agreed immediately, not bothering with the *no, you take the bed* nonsense. His comfort is the least of my concerns.

But I don't go to the bedroom just yet.

Inspired by Mat, I engage in some "crawling and climbing" of my own, starting with the walkout basement and the kitchen. After that I move on to the living room on the ground floor and upstairs to the bedrooms. Knocking gently on one door after another and sneaking in when there's no reply, I cover each level as fast as I can. And as thoroughly as I can. Unlike Mat, my goal isn't to learn how this villa saves energy.

I'm looking for dirt.

Who knows, I may never return to this place, so tonight is my chance to find a room stocked with cocaine packets or a freezer filled with body parts, or at least a bundle of compromising letters.

When I step into a bedroom across the hallway from mine on the first floor, I hear familiar voices and freeze. They're coming from outside. The window is ajar, and the people talking underneath are none other than Darcy and Raphael.

I crouch under the window and listen.

"Your fake girlfriend—she's cute," Raphael says.

"Define cute." Darcy's voice sounds funny. I think he's a little drunk. "Do you mean diverting with her rustic southern accent?"

"No, I mean good-looking."

"Rrrreally?" Darcy slurs. He *is* drunk. "I wouldn't call her good-looking. Perky, yes. Fresh-faced, maybe. But certainly not good-looking."

"You serious?"

"A woman needs a good measure of *class* to be considered good-looking." Darcy pauses before adding, "Diane Petit doesn't have a nanogram of it."

*Ouch*. That stings.

Raphael mutters something and then says louder, "So, under no circumstances would you date her for real?"

I find myself holding my breath.

*Just my vanity, no doubt.*

Darcy takes his time before answering. "I can imagine exactly *three* circumstances where I'd date her for real. First, I go crazy. Can happen to the best of us. Second, I'm coerced. And third, the survival of humanity depends on it."

Raphael chuckles. "Sounds as if you don't have much regard for your future wife."

"It's mutual between us," Darcy says.

*It is, indeed.*

# EIGHT

Earlier today, I woke up to chirping birds and murmuring waves. Darcy was already out. Twenty minutes later, I joined the guests having a sumptuous breakfast on the patio. Their faces showed various degrees of hangover, ranging from Genevieve's zero to Raphael's one hundred with everyone else in between.

I greeted Darcy with the sweetest "good morning, *chéri*" I was capable of and sat down next to Jeanne as the chair next to him was already occupied by Laurent.

*Three cheers for the man!*

A couple of hours later, we arrived in Crete—no sightseeing this time either—and boarded the co-owned jet. At around five in the afternoon, Darcy's chauffeur dropped me off in front of my building, and I was finally home, frustrated and depressed after my luxury getaway.

I feel a lot better now, ensconced in a beauty salon with Elorie, both of us getting massages and manicures.

"So, what's the occasion?" she asks as a nice-smelling lady in a white tunic applies red nail polish to her pinky. "Must be something big."

I focus on my thumb, which is being painted blue. "Why do you say that?"

"You bought me a drink after you got a job offer from that online magazine. Now you're paying ten times more."

I smile and shake my head, still looking for the best way to deliver the bombshell. Elorie will find out about Darcy, anyway, either from a common acquaintance or a photo in a tabloid. It's crucial that I tell her first.

"Did you win the EuroMillions jackpot?" she asks. "That must be it. How much was it?"

I smile. "I won zilch, as usual. But I did sell a few photos through an online depository, and I finally got paid for the wedding I immortalized three weeks ago."

"All right, that explains the *how* of this." Elorie narrows her eyes. "But it doesn't explain the *why*."

OK, Diane—ready, set, roll.

"I've been hiding something important from you," I say. "And now I want to come clean and apologize."

"I knew it!" She let out a smug puff. "Spill the beans."

"I'm seeing someone. And it's getting sort of... serious."

Elorie's jaw slackens. "No way! Since when? Who is he?"

"His name is Sebastian," I say before adding under my breath, "Darcy."

She leans in, eyes wide in disbelief. "Come again—Sebastian who?"

"Darcy."

"Darcy as in d'Arcy du Grand-Thouars de Saint-Maurice, the billionaire count at the helm of Parfums d'Arcy?"

I nod.

"The a-hole who ruined your father?"

"Yes," I mumble.

She turns away and keeps her gaze on her nails for a long moment.

I know what she's itching to say and I dread it.

"Hypocrite," she finally spits out without looking at me.

What can I say in my defense?

Nothing at all.

Elorie pulls a face and says in a squeaky nasal voice, "I'm Saint Diane. I disapprove of your materialistic dream, Elorie. I would never date a billionaire. Money means nothing to me."

Time for another lie. "It's not about his money—I fancy him."

"No kidding." She smirks. "Why would anyone fancy a tall, dark, and handsome billionaire? Who happens to be single. And young."

*And a jerk.*

But that's beside the point.

She purses her lips. "Where did you meet him?"

"He's a friend of Jeanne's husband, Mat."

Elorie blinks. "Jeanne from *La Bohème*?"

"The very same." I take a fortifying breath—here goes one more lie. "It started as casual sex a few weeks ago and grew into something bigger… really fast."

Elorie says nothing.

"Will you forgive me for keeping you in the dark?" I ask.

She keeps silent for a while and then smiles. "Still waters run deep, eh?"

I smile back.

"OK," she says. "I'll forgive you on one condition."

"Shoot."

"Introduce me into his circle."

I grin at Elorie's ever pragmatic attitude. "Consider it done."

"OK," she says. "You're forgiven."

I blow her a kiss.

"Let's rewind to where you said it was getting serious," she says. "What did you mean by that?"

That I'm marrying him in exactly two months.

"Just that we're not hiding anymore, which, by the way, will make it easy to bring you into the fold."

She nods, her eyes bright. I can almost see smoke coming out of her ears as her mind spins with possibilities. Let's hope she meets the man of her dreams through Darcy, so at least someone will have a happy ending when our farce is over.

"Wait," Elorie says. "Will you be quitting the supermarket job?"

I look at my beautifully painted nails. "Why would I do that?"

She shrugs. "Because he can use his connections to get you a better job, dum-dum."

Makes sense, but that's not why I'll quit. I'm going to give in my notice later this week because my contract with Darcy says so.

On page five.

We leave the salon and head to the nearby movie theater for some superhero action accompanied by popcorn and gummy bears.

"Hey, maybe he'll help you become a photographer for fashion magazines," Elorie says with enthusiasm as we slump into our armchairs in the back of the darkened room. "That would be so cool!"

Fashion photography *is* cool, except it isn't my thing. But Elorie's comment reminds me of another matter I wanted to discuss with her.

"I hope I can make it as a photographer on my own," I say. "One of the depositories where I upload my pics asked me for a series of artful portraits in black and white."

She mouths, "Ooh."

"They want tasteful feminine nudes." I hesitate before adding, "Will you pose for me?"

She chokes on her popcorn. "You serious?"

"Yes. You're beautiful and fit, and so much more real than those anorexic fashion models... Not that I'm in a position to ask one to sit for me, anyway."

It's like a lungful of fresh air to be able to say something honest. I'm going to miss that feeling. I already do.

"I'm flattered," Elorie says. "But I have to be careful about my image. Considering my plans."

"Not to worry!" I lean in. "I'll make sure nothing scandalous, such as a nipple, can be seen. The series will be more about the shapes, arches, skin, light, and shadow than about the body."

Elorie chews her lip.

I give her a pleading look. "Please, pretty please?"

"Have you done it before?"

"No," I say honestly. "You'll be my first nude."

"OK," she says. "Why not. Could be fun."

"Thank you, Elorie, you're the best!" I give her a quick hug. "And, by the way, I'll split my fee."

She grins. "Why didn't you start with that, dum-dum?"

*Elorie, you rock.*

When I get home after the movie, my thoughts return to my Greek weekend. Last night, when Darcy walked into our bedroom, I was already under the covers, pretending to sleep. I even produced a loud snore or two for good measure. Because I'm an ace at fake snoring.

And because *I have no class.*

In reality, it took me several hours to fall asleep. I was annoyed with my fruitless search, with Darcy's mean comment, and with the whole fake relationship thing. Suddenly, I was uncertain my plan would work. What if I don't find any incriminating evidence? Maybe Thibaud d'Arcy wasn't murdered. Maybe the family's closets have been purged of all skeletons. Maybe Parfums d'Arcy doesn't sneak carcinogenic components into its flavors and fragrances.

Maybe Sebastian Darcy is the only billionaire in the world who doesn't tuck his money away in offshore accounts.

*Nah, I don't believe that.*

What's more likely, though, is that the money is hidden too well for me to trace.

As our "relationship" is about to go public, some of the implications I've been ignoring hit me hard. Dad will be devastated. He'll be so disappointed he might even stop talking to me. I'll have to lie to him, lie to Mom, Chloe and all my friends. I'll spend the next four to six months pretending I love the man I hate.

And all I'll get out of this may be two hundred grand at best and fifty at worst. If my hidden agenda fails, I won't get any revenge or satisfaction out of this—just money.

It's a terrifying prospect.

# Part III
# Castle

# NINE

March is my least favorite month.

The weather is just as depressing in Paris as it is in Burgundy, London, Montreal, New York, and pretty much everywhere else in the northern hemisphere where I travel for work or leisure. Of course, there's always Tahiti and Australia, but those trips are notorious time eaters. Even Raph's paradisiac Ninossos gets too gray this time of year. Raph doesn't care—he's happy to go there rain or shine, but I'd rather brood in a big city than on a rock in the middle of the sea.

Notice that I haven't done much brooding lately. I've been working my tail off, consolidating the headway Parfums d'Arcy made last quarter and overseeing the launch of three new manufacturing facilities. Not to mention Le Big Ben. Raph and I purchased it last month, and it needs a loving hand to recover its old luster.

Thank God Octave is there—always in good health, remarkably fit and imperturbable—to manage the town house! Because whenever I have a free moment, I spend it with Diane.

That woman makes it virtually impossible to brood even when you're determined to. Not that she makes a special effort to divert me, but she achieves that without meaning to. Sometimes, even despite herself.

Over the past few weeks, she's accompanied me to several society galas and soirées, where we've held hands and smiled for cameras. I've taken her to dinner at exclusive places such as La Tour d'Argent and Jules Verne and for drinks at Royal Monceau and Le Crillon. She didn't seem impressed. I bought a Cartier watch and Chopard earrings for her so she'd look more presentable. She gave me a signed note, saying she'd wear those items while working for me and return them as soon as we were done.

*Strange woman.*

Last week she mentioned she loved musicals, so I flew her to New York to see one on Broadway. She seemed to enjoy herself. But when we returned to Paris, she demanded that I slash the extravagance of my courtship from *overkill* to *gallant*.

Because, she said, she didn't want any perks.

The demand was made just as I was about to hire a personal shopper and a stylist for her. Not because the things she wears are ugly or cheap—which they are, by the way—but because they don't do her justice. Now that I've had ample opportunity to watch and hold her, I *know* she has a delectable figure underneath her sack-like gowns and baggy pants.

And I want to see that figure in a formfitting dress that stops well above the knee.

Beats me why I want that, but I do.

"Diane," I say as I offer my hand to help her out of the car. "You're quitting your job and moving in with me in less than two weeks. You *must* allow me to upgrade your outfits."

She takes my hand and puts a foot on the red carpet rolled out in front of the nightclub. Her delicate foot is shod in a clunky boot, which begs this question—is that all she can afford on her salary or is it what she actually likes? Above the boot, flaps the hem of an ample gown that reminds me of the traditional dress women wear in North Korea. I catch a glimpse of a slim ankle between the boot and the dress, and my fingers burn to touch it. I ignore that urge. It'll pass, eventually. It always does.

"Define *upgrade*," Diane says.

"Let me rephrase it—I'd like to buy you new clothes. And shoes."

"What's wrong with what I wear? Not *classy* enough?"

I hesitate, but only for a second. "Exactly."

Sometimes you have to be blunt to get your message across.

I close the car door behind her and instruct Greg to go home. He argues that he doesn't mind waiting, but I insist. Whether it's out of decency or to avoid Diane calling me a heartless exploiter is an open question.

She's quiet as we enter the club and join my friends partying in one of the larger booths. I decide to drop the subject of her wardrobe.

For now.

With the exception of Laurent, the rest of the company aren't really my *friends* in the original, pre-Facebook sense of the word. They're just people who entertain me enough to spend a couple of hours with them once in a while.

"Hey, look who's here!" Laurent stands to greet us.

The others follow suit, and a few minutes later, my *girlfriend* and I are cozying up to each other in one of the roomy armchairs, sipping our elaborate cocktails.

Unlike the last time I hung out with this group, the conversation is dull, dominated by Jean-François, who can't stop gushing about his new Ferrari. He's been droning on for at least fifteen minutes now, killing Laurent's and his date Yasmina's attempts to change the topic. The women study their nails, and even the men look bored.

"Let's dance," Yasmina says suddenly.

She grabs Laurent's hand and stands up.

"Great idea!" Laurent looks mighty pleased as he follows her to the dance floor.

One by one, the occupants of the booth follow Yasmina's example, and before we know it, it's just Diane, Jean-François, and me. I don't usually dance, but I've heard enough about Ferraris to last me a lifetime. As far as I can tell, so has Diane.

I stand and offer her my hand. "A dance, *chérie*?"

"With pleasure." She gives me a dazzling smile.

Considering the circumstances, she might mean it for once.

Diane isn't a very skilled dancer, but she has a good sense of rhythm, and the way she moves is nice to look at, despite her unfortunate outfit. Something else that's nice to look at are her eyes. Diane is the only person I know whose eyes always hold a private smile. As if she could see something amusing in everything and everyone, at all times. Even when she's angry or sulking, that little smile is still there, illuminating her lovely face and lifting my spirits in a most unexpected way.

A flash of light draws my attention away from Diane's eyes. Ah, paparazzi. I used to turn my back or walk away whenever I spotted one, but these days, their interests and mine are perfectly aligned. I put my hand on the small of Diane's back and draw her closer.

"There's a photo op at three o'clock," I whisper in her ear. "We need to kiss."

"Mild or medium?" she whispers back.

Diane has come up with a four-level Smooch Heat Index to help us navigate the murky waters of pretend affection. Her scale goes from *mild* to *extra hot*. The former is a peck that we use to greet each other and say good-bye in public. *Medium* involves a longer "docking" time and more pressure, but it's still just a brush and our lips remain sealed. I'm allowed to initiate it without asking, albeit a heads-up is always appreciated.

*Hot* corresponds to an openmouthed kiss, suggesting tongue play to an innocent onlooker.

That level requires a prior clearance and is reserved for special occasions. I presume our upcoming betrothal will qualify as such.

Finally, level number four—*extra hot*—is a passionate, shameless kiss, "tongues and all," which she included in her index as a point of reference rather than a workable option. Diane is adamant: *Extra hot* is and will remain out of bounds, unless warranted by exceptional circumstances such as an impending apocalypse or a real danger of exposure.

I cup her cheek and slide my hand to the back of her head. "Hot. We're in a nightclub."

I'm taking a risk here, well aware that a midnight dance can hardly be called a "special occasion." My request isn't justified, and I fully expect her to call my bluff and mouth "no way."

Diane arches an eyebrow as if to say she needs justification.

I just stare at her, holding my ground.

She gives me a small nod.

Before she can change her mind, I pull her into me with my hand at her nape and press my mouth to hers. Every time we kiss, it strikes me how much I enjoy it. My goals, my company, the whole world becomes unimportant as her delicious scent fills my nostrils and the softness of her lips overtakes my mind. So warm, so yielding. I've tried meditating with the best coaches in France and abroad to achieve the state of *mindful relaxation* wherein I empty my head and let go of all my worries.

I swear I have yet to find a shorter path to that coveted state than kissing Diane Petit.

She wraps her arms around my neck, melding her body to mine.

A camera clicks.

I graze her lips and tease them apart.

She lets me. Holding her tight, I stroke her back. My right hand slides to her glorious bottom and stays there, fingers splayed but not daring to squeeze. The temptation to slip my tongue between her soft lips and drink in the taste of her mouth is so strong I can barely resist it.

*No tongues,* I remind myself. She doesn't want tongues. She was very clear on that point.

Diane's hand runs up and down my nape, clutching the back of my neck as if she means it.

*It's just for show. It's just for show. It's just for—*

She removes her hand and draws away.

"We should go," she says.

I'm so drunk on her I need a moment to adjust.

And so does my erection.

She stands on tiptoes and whispers into my ear, "Now, Sebastian. If you grab my hand and we rush out, everyone will think we're running off to fuck."

# TEN

I hail a cab.

"Rue Didot in the 14th," I say to the driver.

Our drill is that I accompany Diane to her place before going home. Sometimes I stay for an hour or so, checking emails on my phone and reading a paper while Diane does chores or edits photos.

She calls that a "quickie."

The few times we've gone to my town house after a date, I've insisted she stay the night, but she always has a good reason to return to her apartment.

As we drive across the city, I'm painfully aware of Diane's thigh next to mine.

*Get a grip, man.*

She isn't even my type. I'm sure I'm reacting this way because I haven't had sex in months, ever since Ingrid left me. That's it; this isn't about Diane, this is just about me having gone too long without a woman. It's decided—I'm getting laid as soon as Diane and I are done, and I won't be picky. The first pretty face who falls into my lap will do just to take the edge off.

Because, heaven help me, that *edge* will be the size of Everest by then.

I stare out the window, surprised to see we're passing by the imposing red gate of the Hôtel d'Hozier and other familiar buildings on rue Vieille du Temple. The taxi is taking us to the left bank through Le Marais. This itinerary is practicable only by night. By day, my neighborhood's mesh of one-way streets makes it a nightmare to drive through.

My town house is just a few blocks away, hidden from sight behind a walled garden, as a self-respecting Parisian *hôtel particulier* should be. It hasn't been in the family for very long—only half a century—but I hope it'll stay for generations to come.

Half an hour later, the cab pulls up outside Diane's building. I pay the driver and follow my intended upstairs.

"I'm not very good with cocktails," Diane says, opening one of her kitchen cabinets. "But I can fix us a gin and tonic."

I sit at the kitchen table. "Sure."

A Scotch is what I'd really like, but I already had two glasses of the best single malt at the nightclub, so I'm fine with a gin and tonic. Or anything, for that matter.

Diane hands me my drink and sits down across from me, nursing her own glass in her hands.

"When you walked me through the contract," she says, "you said something about waiting for 'a certain person to make his move.' "

"Did I?"

She nods. "Did he?"

"Make a move?"

"Uh-huh."

"Not yet."

"What kind of move are we talking about?"

I sigh and spend some time gulping down my drink. Diane is already halfway through her glass.

"My father worshipped my mother," I finally say. "Fifteen years ago, he made a terrible mistake and slept with another woman—a much younger woman, as it happened. She posted their sex tape online the next day."

"She didn't try to blackmail him first?"

"No, and that is additional proof her seduction of Papa was planned by someone who'd paid her."

"A *booty* trap."

I nod.

"Did your dad try to talk to her, find out more?"

"She disappeared."

"And your parents?"

"Maman said he'd broken the sacred vows of marriage and humiliated her. She packed up and left."

"To Nepal?" she asks.

"You're well informed."

She arches an eyebrow. "As your *significant other* and soon-to-be *better half*, it's my duty to be informed."

I guess she has a point. "The first year, she took an apartment in Versailles in Paris, and a year later, she moved to Nepal."

"What's she doing there, by the way?"

"Running a charitable foundation. She hasn't set foot in Paris in years."

"Really?"

I nod. "I was nineteen when she announced she was leaving the country, Raphael fifteen, and Noah only eleven. Raph and I chose to stay here with Papa. Noah went to Nepal with her."

"What happened?"

"Papa... he just... lost his way. Half the time he was depressed, and the other half he tried to *have fun*, often with the help of drugs. Ten years ago, he was found dead."

She nods sympathetically. "Suicide?"

"Overdose, more likely." I shrug. "The report was inconclusive."

"That's a very sad story."

I set my empty glass on the table next to Diane's.

She refills both. "So you believe someone orchestrated the affair that led to his downfall and will now try to do the same to you? Isn't that a bit farfetched?"

I can see how it would seem so.

"A year ago, I met a woman. I really liked her. She came from one of the country's most respectable and wealthiest families, and she was a rare beauty, to boot. We started dating, and things were going in the right direction. She moved in with me. I was thinking of proposing."

She nods as if she already knew this. Well, I guess she might if she reads gossip magazines.

I gulp down half the liquid in my glass and point at Diane's. "You have some catching up to do."

"Oh." She smiles and takes a good swig. "So what happened?"

"I suddenly became terribly popular with gorgeous women."

She cocks her head. "What do you mean by suddenly? You're rich, you're handsome—"

"Wait, did you just call me handsome?"

Diane brings her glass to her face, tips it toward her mouth, and mutters into it, "Did I?"

"I'm positive."

She sets her glass down and puts her chin up in defiance. "So what if I did? You *are* handsome. It doesn't make you a good person."

I suppress a smile, not sure why Diane's admission pleases me so much. "Fair enough."

"Finish your tale," she says.

"Where was I?"

"The Siege of Darcy by Hot Chicks."

"Right. So, all of a sudden, exquisite creatures were wooing me left and right. Naturally, I became suspicious. It was like somebody was trying to stage a remake of my dad's story."

"Or maybe you were just reading too much into someone's flirtation," she says with a wink.

I smirk. "You're right. I'm paranoid. Who would want to hurt me, the harmless do-gooder that I am?"

She doesn't look so amused anymore. I'm sure she's thinking of her father now and what I did to him. It bothers me. I wonder... Does she still hate me as much as she did before I hired her? Or have our conversations and kisses, no matter how fake, mellowed her? Is there a chance she actually enjoys my company?

And my kisses?

She stares at her hands, visibly peeved.

I shouldn't care. She's *not* my girlfriend, not even a friend. It doesn't matter what she thinks of me. It doesn't matter if she likes talking to me or kissing me. It's *strictly business* between us, and it'll stay that way.

"My gut feeling is very trustworthy," I say to break the silence. "And it tells me someone was pulling the strings behind both affairs, Papa's and mine."

"So how did the Siege end?"

"Ingrid grew jealous, and no matter how many assurances of my loyalty I gave her, her trust was broken. She kept saying there's no smoke without fire. It drove me mad."

"You should've told her about your suspicions."

"I did. But she was too far gone. She said I was grasping at straws and inventing ridiculous conspiracy theories to justify my frolicking."

"Because you didn't *frolic* at all, did you?"

"Of course not! I was merely being polite with the ladies." I give her a pointed look. "Anyway, Ingrid and I broke up a few weeks later."

"Who dumped whom?"

I shrug. "She told me she was leaving. I did nothing to stop her."

"I see."

"Miraculously, the lustful supermodels disappeared shortly afterward. Don't you find that strange?"

"Maybe…"

"Anyway, I got over the whole thing more easily than I'd expected. I just plunged into work and moved on."

She smiles. "Your imaginary nemesis must have been disappointed."

"I assure you he or she is very real. But yes, I believe, that person regretted putting things in motion too soon. I'm sure this time he'll wait until I'm married to launch the attack."

"Uh-huh." She looks like she's trying not to smile.

I rub my forehead. "Diane. I know how it sounds. Even Raphael, who witnessed Papa's debacle, isn't fully convinced... But I *know* I'm on to something."

Her expression becomes less amused and more sympathetic.

"Put yourself in my shoes," I continue, eager to capitalize on that seed of sympathy. "Can you imagine how hard it is to suspect everyone around you? And I mean *everyone*—family, friends, relations, help, competitors, subordinates... the whole damn world!"

She nods. "Must be tough."

"I've ruled out a bunch of people, but only Raphael—and now you—knows about my suspicions and my plan. Everyone else must remain in the dark to avoid leaks."

"Makes sense."

Opening up to Diane is a huge relief. Her natural intelligence and inquisitiveness were making it hard for her to play her part without having read the full script. Not that she didn't do a good job, but... let's just say I'm looking forward to having her a hundred percent onboard with this.

"There's someone very dear to me," Diane says, "who's been... troubled for a long time—in a different way than you, but still. She's doing much better now."

*Oh, great.*

She thinks I'm crazy. *Hundred percent onboard,* my foot. Why did I tell her all this? Why didn't I keep my motives secret, as I'd intended? The gin and tonic must have loosened my tongue.

"I'm not *troubled,*" I grate.

"OK." She stares into my eyes. "Whatever you say. I'm just here to do a job and collect my paycheck."

"That's right."

"When do you think your nemesis will make his move?"

"During our honeymoon."

"Why?"

"To be sure to strike while the iron is hot and to maximize the devastating effect it would produce on me."

"What if he decides to wait?"

"He—or she or they—won't. He's running out of time and out of options. With my previous girlfriend, he didn't even wait for us to get engaged."

"And you're sure you'll catch him this time?"

"Oh, yeah. As soon as my new admirer makes an entrance, I'll have a private eye tail her 24-7. I'll be prepared."

She nods.

We finish our drinks in silence.

"You should go home now," Diane says.

She's right.

I pull out my phone and call a cab. I should get some shut-eye. Tomorrow morning, I'll be up at six thirty, as usual. I'll work out for an hour and head to the office. Sleeping in isn't an option. Even on weekends. There are simply too many things to take care of—new markets to conquer, old competitors to decimate, and a backstabbing Judas to unmask.

# ELEVEN

I gasp and forget to shut my mouth.

The view that opens up before me as Greg turns the car from the sinuous countryside road onto a gravel driveway lined with tall oak trees blows my mind. It's early April, and the ancient oaks have fully woken from their winter sleep, their branches spawning clusters of buds and pale green baby leaves. I scoot to the door and peep out the window. On either side of the driveway, green lawns stretch far and wide, smelling of freshly cut grass.

*God, I love that smell!*

We don't have nearly enough of it in Paris.

But it isn't the majestic oak trees or the vast expanses of grass that take my breath away. Set back at the end of the driveway is the Chateau d'Arcy du Grand-Thouars.

A mixture of medieval and Renaissance, the castle reminds me of the Chateau des Milandes in Perigord that I visited with Mom, Dad, Lionel, and Chloe back when Lionel was still in good health. It's smaller, but just as elegant and romantic. As for its grand staircase leading up the main entrance, it totally deserves a red carpet sprinkled with movie stars.

I'm half aware I'm having a most ridiculous Elizabeth-at-the-sight-of-Pemberley moment, but I can't help it. The view is just too damn gorgeous.

And, yes, I'm still a convinced socialist.

And no, I don't think privilege is something people should be born into—it should be obtained based on merit.

And yes, again, I still think that aristocracy with their archaic titles, pompous names, and unwarranted sense of entitlement should be a thing of the past.

But right now, all those righteous thoughts scatter away into the deepest recesses of my brain, letting fascination and awe take center stage.

"What do you think of the castle, mademoiselle?" Greg asks, smiling in the rearview mirror.

I realize my mouth is gaping and quickly shut it, cheeks aflame.

He shifts his gaze to the chateau. "Beautiful, isn't it?"

"It certainly is."

"Monsieur Darcy landed at the Auxerre airport an hour ago. I'm not sure he's at the castle yet."

"He is," I say. "He just texted me. Raphael has been here since last night, and a few other people, too."

"You'll love it here," Greg says.

*I'm not so sure.*

Darcy insisted we spend a long weekend at his ancestral chateau in Burgundy, arguing it would be strange if he didn't bring his soon-to-be fiancée here. Incredible as it may seem, I've never visited this region. Well, now I'm going to get an insider tour of it.

*Aren't I lucky?*

On the program for the weekend is a tour of the castle, its surrounding English-style park, and its wine cellars. We'll also drive through some of the nearby villages and towns and sample their best restaurants. But the highlight of our weekend will be the main local tourist attraction—the Darcy Grotto and its Ice Age rock art.

As soon as Greg stops the car, a youth with a shy smile opens the door for me, mumbling, "Hello, and welcome to the chateau."

Before I can introduce myself, he grabs my overnight bag and rushes inside.

I stare after him, blinking.

"Thank you, Roger," Darcy says to him as the two men pass each other on the staircase, one running up and the other down.

I take in my *boyfriend's* casual look—and quickly avert my gaze. His jeans and fine wool sweater hug his lean, muscular frame in a loose-fitting, conservatively masculine way.

I'm sure he hadn't meant it to be sexy.

Except it is.

He gives me a *mild* kiss. "Did you have a pleasant trip?"

"Oh, come on," I say. "It's just two hours' drive from Paris."

"Could've been an *unpleasant* two hours," he says, arching an eyebrow.

Did he just make a joke? I study his face. His mouth is unsmiling, and there are no laugh lines around his eyes or any other noticeable signs of humor.

Hmm… Hard to tell.

He's been doing this more and more lately— saying things which, coming from any other man, I would immediately recognize as jokes. But from Darcy… he's just not that kind of guy.

Can a man develop a sense of humor after thirty like some develop arthritis or a bald patch?

"Your chateau is awesome," I say.

"It's nothing special, really. There are dozens of similar castles here in Burgundy, and a few are more *awesome* this one. But there's one aspect of it that's unique."

"Which is?"

Darcy lifts a hand, palm up, as if to say, *hang on*. He turns to Greg, who has just parked the Prius between Raphael's flashy red Ferrari and another sports car and now bounds toward us.

"Madame Bruel will show you to your room," he says to Greg. "You're free until Sunday evening."

"*Merci*, Sebastian. I have some friends in Auxerre. It'll be great to see them."

"Take the Prius—I'll be driving the Lamborghini." Darcy turns back to me. "What's unique about this castle is that it's never changed hands. It was built by Chevalier Henri d'Arcy du Grand-Thouars at the end of the sixteenth century."

"Oh, my God!" I clap my hand to my mouth. "And he still owns it? Is he a ghost? Does he have chains? Can I meet him?"

Darcy's lips twitch and form that crooked, unpracticed smile of his that I hate because of what it does to my insides.

"What I meant," he says, "is that the castle has remained in the family. Its current owner is my brother Noah."

"Is he here? Am I finally going to meet him?"

"No. He—"

"Couldn't make it," I finish for Darcy.

Noah never makes it to any party or event organized by his older brothers—not even when said event is held at his own castle. Neither does Darcy's mother, by the way. But she, at least, has the excuse of living in Nepal.

Darcy's expression hardens.

"Let me get this straight," I say to lighten things up. "You don't own the island, you only co-own the jet and the club, and now you tell me the castle isn't yours, either."

"That's correct."

I arch an eyebrow. "And here I thought I was snatching a *real* billionaire."

"You are." He smiles again. "I inherited Parfums d'Arcy, which is worth well over a billion. It's one of Europe's largest individually owned businesses. Not to mention the trinkets such as the Paris town house and apartments in London and New York."

The expression of genuine pride on his face is the same as the one I saw on Liviu—Jeanne's friend's nine-year-old—last Wednesday. He'd dragged his mom to *La Bohème* so he could show everyone his new remote control toy drone.

As the saying goes, the only difference between men and boys is the price of their toys.

"Oh, good." I exhale in feigned relief. "I was almost about to call the whole marriage thingy off."

As we reach the top of the stairs and step inside, a skinny woman in her fifties holds her hand out. "I'm Jacqueline Bruel, the housekeeper."

I shake her hand. "Diane. Very pleased to meet you."

"The pleasure is all mine," she says with a sincere smile before pointing to a wide wooden staircase across the foyer. "My office is on the first floor, second door on the left. Knock if you need anything. Or give me a call."

She turns to Darcy, raising an eyebrow in half question.

"I'll make sure Diane has your number, Jacqueline," he says, leading me upstairs.

Unlike the sleek villa on Ninossos and the impeccably kept town house, the castle looks as if it has seen better days. Everything in here is authentic and beautiful—but also threatening to collapse at any moment.

The antique ceiling fixtures will be the first, I'm sure, followed by the creaky floorboards under our feet.

"Needs work, huh?" Darcy says, following my gaze.

I nod.

"I almost approached Chloe a month ago, seeing how tastefully and respectfully she rehabbed *La Bohème*, but..." He sighs. "This chateau is Noah's. He needs to at least confirm he wants it restored."

When we reach the second floor, Darcy opens a door, which groans and nearly unhinges itself in protest, to a spacious room.

"The lord and lady's chamber," he says. "Aka our bedroom. The bathroom is two doors to the right."

I step inside and take in the large four-poster, the exquisite Art Nouveau wardrobes and chests of drawers, and the mildew stains on the walls. The wood floor is covered with beautiful rugs, their blue flower patterns in perfect harmony with the rest of the decor.

I look around for the couch area like the one in the town house, but don't find one.

Darcy points to a small door between the wardrobes. "There's an adjacent room right there. Grandpapa Bernard and Grandmaman Colette, who were the last ones to refurbish the castle, slept in separate bedrooms."

"How clever of them," I say, my shoulders slacking with relief. "So, who's around? I saw Raphael's car outside. Anyone else I know?"

"Genevieve—you met her at his birthday party. We're also hosting Dr. Muller, the archeologist who manages the Grotto, and the mayor of the village with his spouse. You'll meet everyone at dinner tonight."

Ah, I see. The cream of the local society.

What a shame Elorie couldn't be here today! She had to stay in Paris for her dad's fiftieth birthday party. But she's coming over tomorrow morning, and Darcy and I will fetch her from the train station.

I can't wait.

"The dinner will be served at eight in the great hall, but at four, we all meet in the front yard to visit the cave." Darcy heads for the little door. "I'll let you freshen up."

"What's the dress code?"

The dos and don'ts of high society go over my head, so I always prefer to ask.

"Casual." He hesitates for a second and adds, "*My* casual."

*Ha!*

This is Darcy's way of admitting that what passes for casual in his circles, normal people call dolled up. *My* casual for midseason consists of well-worn baggy jeans and a roomy sweater. I wore the combo to a couple of *informal* outings with Darcy's friends. Only everyone else looked as if they'd read the wrong memo and had dressed for a job interview at *Vogue*.

When Darcy raised the matter of buying me clothes again a couple of weeks ago, I promised I'd make an effort. And I did. I bought a pair of jeans and two sweaters from a low-cost supermarket.

At least they were new.

In regards to the formal events that require gowns, I've found a solution that eliminates an extra expenditure from Darcy or me.

I borrow.

Elorie and I are the same size, and my initial idea was to ask for one or two of her little black dresses that would be perfect for any occasion. But something stopped me. It may have to do with the way Darcy looks at me, especially when I show some skin or wear pants that are a notch tighter than my norm.

It may also have to do with the way my stupid body reacts to those looks.

So instead of Elorie's sexy LBDs, I picked a few of Manon's formless gowns she's kept from her XL days as a reminder of what awaits her if she puts on weight again. Those gowns swallow me up, their thick material creating a shield-like barrier between me and Darcy. They're my chastity belts of sorts. And while it annoys and saddens me that I need one around Darcy, I'm not taking any risks. I haven't even moved in with him yet, for crying out loud.

Hmm, I wonder if there's an online shop that carries a high-tech twenty-first-century version of a *real* chastity belt... Perhaps I should order one.

Just in case.

# TWELVE

Dr. Muller, whom I imagined to be an old gentleman with a white beard and a cane, is in fact a pretty woman in her early thirties. With a powerful flashlight in her hand, she gives us a private tour of the Darcy Grotto, a large complex of interconnected caves just a fifteen-minute walk from the castle.

Under normal circumstances, anyone can visit the Grotto even if, like most caves in France, it's on private land. We follow Dr. Muller through stalactite galleries and halls. Here and there, icicle-like stalactites meet with stalagmite mounds in passionate embraces. They're called columns, Dr. Muller explains.

We're headed to the Mammoth Hall, which hosts the oldest prehistoric rock paintings in France.

Dr. Muller says they're forty thousand years old.

As we trek behind her, I can't help thinking she looks like someone you'd expect to tread catwalks, rather than cave galleries, for a living. Her knee-length trench coat and snug little boots do a great job of drawing the eye to her slender and exceptionally well-shaped legs. I bet Darcy is ogling them right now.

Even I—a one hundred percent heterosexual woman—am ogling them right now.

There's no denying Dr. Muller is the bomb. She's smart, good-looking, and classy. Unlike the *perky* me, who doesn't have a *nanogram* of class, according to my future ex-husband.

Why didn't he ask *her* to be his fake girlfriend?

Maybe he's reserving her for when the coast is clear of his nemesis and he can have a real relationship with a suitable woman.

"*Et voilà*," Dr. Muller says, turning around. "We've reached the Mammoth Hall. I invite everyone to study the ceiling and the walls."

Striking images of mammoths, lions, and reindeer painted in ochre and charcoal adorn the cave. They're simple and yet perfectly drawn, the animals full of grace and easy to recognize despite minimal detail.

"I don't see any rabbits or foxes," Raphael says. "Why's that?"

Dr. Muller smiles. "The Paleolithic Man didn't draw the animals he hunted."

"So these paintings had a ritualistic function?" Genevieve asks.

"We believe so." Dr. Muller brushes a strand of hair from her face with the elegance of a ballerina. "But the truth is we don't really know."

I raise my hand. "Did you find any paintings of people?"

"We found a few representations of women. But no men. That is, no complete men."

"What do you mean?" Raphael asks.

"I mean this." She points her torchlight to a familiar-looking drawing on the ceiling.

I peer and realize it's an erect penis. Or, should I say in this context, a *phallus*.

I give Darcy a wink. "A forty-thousand-year-old cock and balls graffiti, huh? Some things never change."

Just before we climb out of the cave, I spot a distinctly Asian sculpture submerged up to its neck in a small pond formed by water dripping from the ceiling. It looks completely out of place in this prehistoric cave.

"Oh, it's a Buddha," Dr. Muller says matter-of-factly, following my gaze.

I stare into her eyes. "A Buddha."

She nods.

I clap my hand to my forehead. "But of course— stupid me! It's *the* famous Ice Age Bathing Buddha of Burgundy."

Darcy grins.

He actually stretches his lips and opens his mouth wide enough for this smile to qualify as a full-fledged grin, the first one I've ever seen on him.

It nukes me to a pile of rubble.

"I can explain," he says. "The Buddha is on loan from Le Louvre. The curators there wanted to see what the special variety of bacteria in this pool will do to him."

"He's been here for fifteen years now," Dr. Muller says.

I turn to her. "And?"

"Nothing." She spreads her hands. "No effect whatsoever."

"You need to have a word with your bacteria," I say to my *beau*. "Le Louvre counts on them."

"Oh, that reminds me!" Dr. Muller scurries over to Darcy. "I must discuss an urgent matter with you."

"Of course," he says. "We'll talk after dinner."

She adds something in a hushed voice, clearly unwilling for anyone to overhear. Must be business related, I tell myself. And confidential. Maybe she caught someone on the team cheating or she wants to negotiate an additional guide position.

Regardless, I'm rattled… and annoyed for being rattled.

But then I catch Genevieve watching me watch Dr. Muller talking with Darcy. Am I being prejudiced and way off the mark to read her expression as gloating?

Elorie can't come here soon enough.

# THIRTEEN

At dinner, I meet the mayor, who's adorable with his seventies mustache and a polo shirt tucked into his old-fashioned jeans. His wife wears a pink tweed jacket and has an easy laugh. We get on immediately and chat away for most of the meal.

Just as I begin to tell myself this evening isn't as bad as I'd expected, Darcy invites the guests to move to the drawing room for a more relaxed second part of the soirée. Darcy and Dr. Muller walk over to the window and launch into a long conversation. Genevieve expertly maneuvers the mayor's wife away from me to the other sofa across a ginormous coffee table.

"Did you like the cave?" she asks.

Something tells me she doesn't really care. Her question is just an opener for something else.

"It was impressive," I say honestly. "I loved the paintings and I learned a lot."

She inches a little closer. "Isn't Penelope—that's Dr. Muller's first name—amazing?"

*Et voilà.* "She sure is."

"Such competence, such drive! You know, she comes from a long pedigree of writers and academics."

"Good for her."

"Penelope and I are very close," she says. "I have so much respect for her achievement. In my eyes, it's more important than money or titles."

She gives me a long, intense stare as if trying to gauge if the penny has dropped.

I'm itching to say, *Hey, I get it, despite my limited education. You're reminding me I have neither merit nor money, not to mention a title. You're suggesting I'm the odd one out in this room. But you know what? We're in agreement. I don't belong here, and I sure as hell don't want to belong. If I weren't bound by a contract, I'd be hanging out with Elorie and Manon at* La Bohème *instead of wasting precious minutes of my life listening to your aristocratic farts. They stink just the same as everyone else's.*

Unfortunately, I can't say any of it.

Damn that contract!

This is the hardest I've bitten my tongue in the past two months. There've been other temptations, but none of them this strong. Genevieve has been cold and indifferent, but not mean. Neither have any of Darcy's other acquaintances. Most of them just try to be friendly without realizing they're patronizing me. When we chat, they avoid long words. They find me "cute." In their eyes, I'm Darcy's long-overdue fling with a plebeian. They consider our *amourette* as his rite of passage, his brave—and brief—exploration of the world of commoners.

And I'm forced to put up with that shit.

If there's one reason I look forward to Darcy's announcement of our betrothal, it's to see the look on their faces at that moment. Especially on Genevieve's.

My peripheral vision catches Darcy's shape looming next to us.

"Can I steal my girlfriend for a moment?" he asks Genevieve.

"Of course." She gives him a canned smile. "You can sit here—I was going to go chat with Raphael, anyway."

Darcy puts his glass on the coffee table and sits next to me. "I hope you enjoyed your first day at the castle."

"I did," I say. "Up until ten minutes ago."

He doesn't ask why. Instead, he takes my hand and holds it with both his. I lift my gaze to his face. He's staring at me with an intensity that would've stopped my heart under different circumstances. *Wow*. Anyone looking at him right now would say he's crazy for me. Even I have to remind myself he's just playing a part.

And he's damn good at it, just like everything he does.

Hmm, let's see if I can match his skill. I peer into his dark brown eyes, remarking a hue in them I hadn't noticed before. It's amber gold. In fact, it's the exact color of the Scotch he was sipping before he sat down.

Will I taste it on his tongue if we kiss?

Right on cue, he leans in for a smooch, and I whisper "*extra hot*" before I can stop myself. Surprise flickers in his eyes. A split second later, he angles his head and slants his mouth over mine. His evening stubble grates against my chin in a most pleasant way. He runs his tongue over my lips and nips gently. I open up. His tongue penetrates deep inside between my teeth, against my palate and my cheeks, pushing against my own tongue.

He thrusts, strokes and suckles, giving my mouth the most sensual, shameless treatment it's ever had.

He's making love to it.

Desire shoots to my core in a lightning bolt of unspeakable sweetness. I find myself leaning into him, opening up more, asking for more. Me, who despises couples who can't restrain their ardor in public—I can't get enough of him at this moment, public opinion be damned.

He tastes of whisky and of something quintessentially male. That taste, combined with his head-turning scent, is nudging me into an unfamiliar territory that borders on total abandon. My breasts ache for his hand to cup and fondle them. As for his other hand, I want it between my legs.

I *need* it between my legs.

There's only one word to qualify the effect of this kiss—madness.

I'm losing my fucking mind.

And I don't even care.

Just as abruptly as he started the kiss, Darcy stops and draws away.

I gasp for air and open my eyes.

He's watching me. There's no more playfulness nor the slightest shade of amber left in his eyes. His gaze is dark, and his lips are red from our kiss.

He turns away and says something to the person on his right.

I blink to clear the haze from my eyes and focus on the man he's talking to.

It's Raphael.

My hearing returns next, and with it, a profound sense of embarrassment.

"I'll talk to him first thing Monday morning," Raphael says.

Darcy nods. "Be sure that you do."

Next to Raphael, Genevieve studies my face, barely pretending to listen to what her "very close" friend Penelope is saying to her.

Penelope glances at her watch and stands. "I should be going."

"You should stay," Darcy says. "It's late, and there are plenty of empty bedrooms in this castle."

She hesitates. "The village is only twenty minutes away. I'll be fine—I'm a big girl."

"Penelope." There's a bossy note in Darcy's voice. "I don't like the idea of you driving alone on dark countryside roads at this hour."

She stares at him, saying nothing.

"You'll sleep at the castle." He pulls out his phone. "I'll let Jacqueline know, so she can get you everything you need."

"That's very kind of you, Sebastian." Penelope smiles. "Thank you."

I approve of his thoughtful gesture, but I can't help wishing Penelope had refused. The thought of her sleeping in one of the guest chambers under the same roof as Darcy is unpleasant to say the least.

Is he going to join her later tonight, so that they could continue their *conversation*?

No, he won't. He'd never do anything that could blow our cover. This scheme of his matters too much to him.

Just as I sigh with relief, a thought strikes me.

*I'm jealous.*

Why else would I care if Darcy and Penelope spend the night together?

*Chill out, woman.*

What you're experiencing is a version of Stockholm syndrome, when hostages end up supporting the bad guy because they've spent too much time in close proximity with him. The difference between the classic version of the syndrome and mine is that instead of sympathizing with Darcy's cause, I've become sympathetic toward his body. Fervently sympathetic.

No, this won't do.

Repeat after me, Diane: *Darcy is an entitled jerk. He ruined and nearly killed Dad. It's sick to lust after him while plotting his downfall. My dream is to see him destroyed.*

Excellent.

And now the refrain.

*I hate him.*

*I hate him.*

*I hate him.*

# FOURTEEN

Elorie's skin glows in the soft light filtering through the tall linen-draped window of this high-ceilinged room.

I fiddle with the controls of my camera. "Can you tip your head back a little?"

"Like this?" Elorie asks.

"Exactly." I release the shutter. "Don't move."

She's straddling a polished wood chair, her back toward me. The paleness of her skin is offset by the dark wood of the chair and the floorboards. I study the image on my preview screen. It's elegant and free of any vulgarity, yet there's a touch of delicious decadence you can't miss. It's perfect, thanks to this light and this space. If I could afford a professional studio for my portraits, I doubt I could find a better setting.

I click a few more times, gleeful.

This is going to be the best of the three shoots we've done so far. It has everything going for it. Especially three things—Elorie's lovely body, the shabby-chic charm of this room, and our mojo boosted by the best local Chablis from Darcy's wine cellar.

"More?" I ask, picking up the bottle.

She grabs her glass from the floor and holds it out. "Yes, please. When do you think you'll be done?"

"I *am* done, actually." I fill her glass and hand it to her. "I was going to take a few more pics, just in case. But if you're tired or cold, we can stop now."

Before she replies, the door behind me opens and Darcy walks in. Surprise flashes in his eyes as he takes in the scene. He looks ragged with ruffled hair, dark stubble, and a glass of Scotch in his hand. Combined with the jeans and a well-worn sweater, the look is so out of character I can't help wondering if he's OK.

Then I remember about Elorie and panic.

The poor thing must be mortified. Oh, and she'll kill me as soon as she gets over it. Our shoots were supposed to remain secret, and no one was supposed to know it was her in these photos.

"Get out!" I shout at Darcy.

"I didn't mean to intrude." He turns toward my model, his gaze trained on the floor next her feet. "Please forgive me, Elorie."

"It's OK," she says.

He glances at me again as he retreats toward the door. "I hope I didn't ruin your project. Please continue."

I glare at him.

And to my utter shock, my naked friend turns around, fully exposing to Darcy all her X-rated parts she's been so eager to hide from my camera. "Hi, Sebastian."

His lips quirk before he schools them into a polite smile. "Hello, Elorie."

She picks up her bathrobe and pulls it on. "We were done, actually and I was leaving. So no worries—you didn't ruin anything."

"I'm glad to hear it," he says.

"See you later, alligator." Elorie waves good-bye to me.

"I'll get you before the restaurant," I say as she makes a beeline to the door and shuts it behind her.

"You never told me you did nude portraits," Darcy says.

I shrug. "Our contract doesn't require that I tell you everything."

"Do they sell well?"

"Elorie and I are on our third series," I say with pride. "So yeah, my nudes seem to be appreciated."

He points at my camera. "Can I see one?"

My first impulse is to say no, but I remember Elorie's cavalier attitude and change my mind. Compared to the uncensored view she just presented him, my photos are PG-13.

I hand him the camera.

As he pulls up the pics, I survey him. What would he look like naked? I saw his biceps once when he wore a T-shirt. I've leered at the bulges of his pecs discernible through his shirts countless times. His stomach is flat, his shoulders are naturally broad, and his hips narrow. All evidence suggests he'd look very nice indeed. What I don't know is if his chest is hairy. I picture his bared forearms as an indicator. Hmm… it'll probably have some hair, but not too much. If I find the right aperture and exposure settings to accentuate the play of light and shadow on the planes of his chest, I could have some amazing photos.

"Will you sit for me?" I blurt.

He gives me a quizzical look.

"As in pose for a few pics… maybe?" I fully expect him to snort and say no.

He tilts his head to the side. "Are you serious?"

*Am I?* "Totally."

"Why? Are you having trouble finding male models?"

"I haven't tried. You'd be my first."

He glances at the preview screen once again.

I should stop holding my breath. He'll never agree to my brazen offer. No way.

"So you want me to pose for you," he says.

"Uh-huh."

"Naked?"

I nod. "I'll make them just as clean and artsy as Elorie's. And I'll hide your face by shooting from the side and the back only."

He hands me the camera, a smile crinkling his eyes. "Only for art's sake…"

Is he agreeing to my insane request? Is he actually, really, going to do it?

I clear my throat. "Is that a yes?"

He doesn't reply immediately, and I stare at him, a wave of shameful, giddy excitement shooting through my veins, filling my ears with a pleasant buzz and making me light-headed. Darcy is going to strip naked for me. He's going to position that gorgeous body of his however I instruct him to. I'm going to be able to feast my eyes on every inch of that taut, virile flesh with full impunity. Pretending to be just an extension of my camera and safe in the artist-model role-play, I'm going to lap up every line of that handsome face. It's shocking how badly I want him to say yes.

"One condition," he says. "I keep my pants on."

I do my best to hide my disappointment. "OK, but only the pants. I want your chest and your feet bare."

He nods.

"I'll prepare the backdrop while you undress." I try to sound businesslike. "We have to hurry—this light will be gone in twenty minutes or so."

He sets his glass on the windowsill and pulls his sweater over his head with the ease of a hunk who doesn't know what body-conscious means.

I don't budge, watching him.

He kicks off his sneakers, eyes riveted to mine.

I stare, mesmerized into a stupor.

His pulls his socks off and straightens his back. "Weren't you going to prep something?"

"What?" I wake up from my trance. "Oh. Crap. Yes, I was." I rush past him to move the chair out of the way and push the curtain a little to the side. My ears are aflame.

"Can you stand by the window?" I ask.

Without looking at him, I go back to my spot by the table and pick up my camera.

Darcy plants himself on the right of the window frame. His upper body is to die for. All lean muscle and tanned skin. Incredibly masculine. Totally camera worthy. Oh, and I was right about his chest, which has just the right amount of hair.

"Press your forehead to the frame," I say.

He executes.

*Click, click, click.*

"Now turn your back to me, lift your arms, and place your hands on either side of the frame."

He does as he's told.

"Higher. Yes, like that. Lean forward a bit. Perfect. Stay there."

I click frantically.

"Drop your head to your chest… Good… Now, straighten up again. Drop your right hand behind your neck and touch your back… Beautiful."

I order him to shift his body in a dozen more ways, each designed to highlight a particular group of muscles on his back and chest, the slant of his shoulders, the shape of his strong neck, his sculpted jawline, abs, hips, backside, and his unexpectedly sexy feet.

Male beauty is *so* underrated.

"How about a nude?" I ask on impulse. "Just one pic, to crown the series."

He stares at me, saying nothing.

His silence emboldens me. "I'll take it from the back, nothing indecent, and I'll render it in black and white. Please?"

He stare grows so intense it robs me of air. Literally. It somehow makes me unlearn the art of breathing, and I'm about to swoon when he nods and turns his back to me.

I take a few life-saving breaths.

He just nodded, right? He's going full monty for me.

*Dear God, dear God, dear God.*

Incredulous, I watch him unbuckle his belt and draw the zipper. In one smooth movement, he pulls his jeans and underwear down and steps out of them.

My gaze travels up his athletic calves and strong thighs and lingers on his derriere. A part of me registers that I'm staring at him directly without the intermediary of the camera.

Another part registers that I'm wet.

"So?" Darcy asks without turning to face me. "Are you taking that shot?"

I raise the camera and click, and click again, and again, and again.

"That's more than one pic," he says.

"It's just to have a few different angles to choose from."

*And look at.*

"We're done," I say a moment later. "It was very kind of you, Sebastian."

"Don't mention it." I hear the smile in his voice. "I'm glad I could be of help, Diane."

I turn to the door, hugging my camera. "I'll give you some privacy to get dressed."

"That would be nice. Thank you."

As I march out and pull the door closed, I already know I'm going to spend hour after hour pouring over the series, inventing new ways to edit the photos just to have an excuse to leer at them.

Especially, the last few.

# FIFTEEN

Hating a man 24-7 drains your energy. Can you blame a woman for needing a break from it?

That's what this is—a break. Whenever I find myself enjoying Darcy's company, I tell myself that all it means is that I'm just taking a breather from constant hating. Neat, huh? In this light, there's no reason to panic every time I catch myself fancying Darcy's toothsome bod or admiring a trait of his character.

This theory is the *only* way to account for what happened in Burgundy. Prompting Darcy to give me an *extra hot* kiss was bad enough. I can tell myself I did it to spite Genevieve, who'd gotten under my skin, but how do I explain that I nearly disintegrated from it? And how in hell do I explain asking Darcy to strip and pose for me? A fit of madness? An attempt to sabotage my own plan? An admission of defeat?

I prefer to go with the *Everyone Needs a Breather* hypothesis.

Anyway, back to the here and now. I'm standing next to Jeanne in the middle of the front room of *La Bohème*, staring at the long windowless wall opposite the entrance. At Jeanne's request, Chloe had fitted it with little hooks and strings so it could serve as a gallery to showcase local painters.

"Your photos of Parisian rooftops would be perfect for my first exhibit," Jeanne says.

"I'm flattered,"—and I truly am—"but I wouldn't want you to feel obligated to offer me this opportunity just because I'm Chloe's sis."

"I'm offering you this opportunity because I love those photos, period." Jeanne cocks her head and winks. "But don't expect me to pay for the prints."

"Are you insane? *You* should be charging me, not the other way around!"

We agree on the size and number of prints, and Jeanne returns behind the bar. I stare at the wall some more, brimming with excitement. Displaying my work outside the virtual world, printed and framed, is a big step toward becoming a real photographer. It doesn't matter how many photos I sell—this exhibit isn't about making a profit. It's my graduation from hobbyist to professional.

Manon zooms by with a loaded tray, mouthing, "Five minutes." This means she's about to take a coffee break and wants me to stick around. I pick a table by the window and engross myself in my current whodunit.

Manon's voice pulls me out of the story a few minutes later. "How can you enjoy that stuff?"

"What's wrong with detective stories?"

She sits down, placing a cappuccino and an espresso on the table. "All that violence and crime."

"To me, these books are more about the intrigue and figuring out who the culprit is." I cock my head. "What *I* don't understand is how you can like romance."

"What's not to like?" She gives me a dreamy look. "I can never decide what I enjoy more—the thrill of the deepening love, the overcoming of obstacles, or the guaranteed happily ever after."

"There are no happily ever afters in real life."

"If you mean we all die in the end, I agree." She gives me a wink. "But romance books aren't about eternal life. They're about eternal love."

"Does it exist, your eternal love?" I sneer.

She stares at me, perplexed. "You just got engaged. Shouldn't you be a little more... optimistic?"

"I should—I mean, I am." I glance at the ridiculously big diamond on my finger. "It's just… People come together and split up. Or they stay together and hate each other's guts. That's real life— just look around you."

"OK." She nods, a sparkle of mischief in her eyes, and turns toward the bar. "Let's see… Oh, look, it's Jeanne!"

Manon turns back to me, beaming.

I know exactly what she's going to say.

"Last time I checked,"—she can hardly keep the glee from her voice—"Jeanne was still happily in love with Mat."

I shrug. "They're an exception to the rule."

"What about Chloe and Hugo?" Manon arches an eyebrow. "How long will you give those two?"

Hmm. Very long, actually. Until death do them part.

"My parents divorced," I say. "So did Sebastian's, and Elorie's, and plenty of other people I know."

"OK, I'll grant you that," Manon says. "Not *every* couple gets their happily ever after. In real life, half of them split up."

"Ha! You see."

"But the other half stays together and continues loving each other, just like in romance books. And lots of divorcees remarry happily." She pats my shoulder. "It's one of those glass-half-full things— just a matter of perspective."

"Or a matter of dumb luck."

"Maybe." She rubs her chin. "Or maybe it's a matter of knowing yourself well enough to sense who's right for you."

"How can you ever sense that? It's not as if there's an alarm in your head that goes"—I cup my hands around my mouth—"weeeoooo-weeeoooo, all systems go! I have a visual. The individual at three o'clock is the perfect match. I repeat: Target at three o'clock. Go, go, go!"

"That's not how it works." She smiles and glances at fellow waiter Amar as he walks by eyeing Manon as if she were the Eighth Wonder of the World. "You don't always recognize it at once, but when you've spent some time with the right guy, you'll know it's him. Trust me."

Lucky her. I've never felt that confident about anyone.

I guess I don't know myself well enough.

# SIXTEEN

Denying yourself someone you crave, and who happens to want you, too, drains your energy. Can you blame a man for wanting a break from it?

I'd been suspecting Diane had a thing for me since March, but the Burgundy trip killed the last of my doubts. I'll never forget our *extra hot* kiss, or the look on her face when she asked me to pose for her. Even harder to forget is the giddiness in her lovely eyes when I agreed. Not to mention the pent-up lust roughening her voice when she directed me, and the color of her cheeks when she began to take pictures.

How I managed not to knock on her door that night is beyond me.

I look out the car window as I drive to the 9th. I'm to join Diane and her gang at *La Bohème* tonight, where they're watching some show on the bistro's new TV screen. My original plan had been to take Diane to the opera, but she said she wouldn't miss that program for the world.

Why on earth did I buy those tickets without checking with her first? I suppose I was going for a surprise. As if I didn't already know Diane isn't the kind of woman who'd jump for joy at two center orchestra tickets for *La Traviata*.

I smirk and shake my head.

*She's the exact opposite.*

Setting aside the women who live in mud huts on under one dollar a day, Diane is as far from my interests and way of life as a Western female can be. And that's why I stayed away from her chamber in Burgundy. Just imagine the imbroglio of having sex with the woman I've hired to play my fiancée. *Hired* and *play* are the keywords here. Sleeping with her might give Diane the wrong idea. And if there's one thing a gentleman never does to a woman—regardless of her social background—is giving her the wrong idea.

*Hang in there, man.*

Just two more months of this charade and she'll be out of my life for good.

I park the Lambo on the corner of rue Lafayette and rue Bleu and climb out.

As I walk down rue Cadet, I notice an unusually large crowd blocking the sidewalk terrace of the bistro. It's early May, and mild enough to sip your *Kir cassis* outside, but that doesn't explain all those extra chairs, people standing in the aisles, and others sitting on their backpacks. And everyone—everyone—has their heads turned up, staring at the wall-mounted TV.

Diane, Elorie, Jeanne, and some of the waiters are among the crowd. My fiancée remains seated as I peck her on the forehead. She's wearing the perfume I gave her a few weeks ago, and this pleases me to no end. The delicate iris- and patchouli-based fragrance blends seamlessly with the alluring scent of her skin, highlighting her tomboyishness as well as her femininity.

I wish I could bottle it and keep it in my inside pocket at all times.

When my mind clears a few seconds later, I say hello to the others. They greet me without taking their eyes off the screen.

Is there some important match underway? Why didn't Octave or Greg tell me anything? They're both huge sports fans and between them, they have all major sports covered. So what is it—tennis, football, or rugby?

The screen displaying country names and points isn't helping.

"What are you watching?" I ask.

"The Eurovision Song Contest," Diane says before turning to her friends. "This can't be true! Belgium gave us *nul points*. How could they?"

Manon grits her teeth. "Traitors."

"So did the UK," Elorie says.

"Yeah, but that's normal." Diane looks at me. "It's a tradition. Brits always down vote France at *Eurovision*. We do the same to them, by the way."

I place my hand on her shoulder.

Diane gives me a sweet smile. "Will you stay and watch this with us?"

"I was hoping to take you to dinner—I haven't eaten yet. Besides,"—I look around—"there are no spare chairs."

"I can fix you a *croque-monsieur* or a hamburger," Jeanne offers.

Diane stands and pats her chair. "We can share this."

"OK." I sit down and turn to Jeanne. "A hamburger and a beer would be great."

She stands. "Don't let anyone steal my chair."

"I'll guard it with my life." Diane drops her purse on it.

"So, let's see what's this all is about," I say to Diane, as she lowers herself onto my lap.

This song contest is clearly something she enjoys. I'm not going to spoil her evening by insisting we go eat a proper dinner in a proper restaurant. And I wouldn't want to appear rude by leaving. So my reasons for staying are just gallantry and good manners. And perhaps curiosity about this European song contest I've heard about but never watched.

The prospect of having Diane's pert little ass on my lap and my arm wrapped around her slim waist for the next hour or so has nothing to do with anything.

"Who's the favorite?" I ask. "Are they good?"

Diane picks up her mojito. "Malta and Ukraine are number one and two, but it may change with the next country's vote."

"Everyone's equally awful in this contest," Elorie says.

"Then why watch it?"

"The point of watching the Eurovision Song Contest," Diane says, "isn't in discovering good songs or new talent—we have *The Voice* for that. It's in commenting."

"On what?"

Diane turns to me. "Everything. The contestants and their costumes, the hosts and their bad jokes, and, of course, the songs."

"You forgot the national commentators," Elorie says. "We comment on them, too." She turns to me. "This year it's your buddy, celebrity columnist Marie-Anne Blenn."

"She's not my buddy."

Elorie cocks her head. "But you've met her, haven't you?"

"Everyone with a 'de' particle in their name has met her."

Manon puts her index finger to her lips. "Shush! Australia is next."

"I thought this was a European contest," I can't help saying.

"Didn't you watch the news last night?" Jeanne puts my hamburger and beer on the table and takes her seat. "Australia was hauled across a couple of oceans and parked between Iceland and Scotland so they could take part in *Eurovision*."

"Shush!" Manon orders again.

We watch the song that's so resolutely and proudly tacky it deserves at least one point. To my surprise, it gets a lot more than one, including from France. Have my fellow citizens lost their famed good taste? A longtime opera buff, I forget that the vast majority of the seventy million people who are just as French as I am wouldn't set foot in an opera house even if I paid them.

The next performer has the left side of his skull shaven and the right side covered in long raven-black strands that drape his right eye like a little curtain.

"The Barber from Hell has struck again," Marie-Anne Blenn's voice-over informs the viewers.

"Wait till he starts singing," Manon says. "I've already watched his video on YouTube. His song is called 'Eagle.' "

Diane tilts her head back and looks up. "Lord, please make it so that he doesn't have wings attached to his back."

Manon purses her lips, struggling not to smile.

The singer opens his mouth—and spreads his eagle wings.

Diane drops her head to her chest. Manon giggles.

A well-endowed female singer dressed in a long skirt and tight bodice steps out from behind a curtain. Ten seconds into her tear-jerking song, she raises her arms to the ceiling, clenches her fists and rips off her skirt.

"She has the male vote in her pocket," Elorie says.

Diane turns to her. "She doesn't have any pockets."

"Fine. Tucked into her bodice." Elorie pokes her tongue out. "Smartass."

And so it continues. Song after cheesy song gets points following a logic I fail to grasp. One thing is clear—it has nothing to do with their artistic quality.

At some point, I realize I'm staring at the screen without seeing anything. Nor am listening to Marie-Anne Blenn's and the girls' acerbic comments. My mind is completely overtaken by something a lot closer to home—Diane. More specifically her back against my chest, my left hand on her tummy, and my right hand, which has somehow made its way to her thigh.

I'm sporting wood. And I'm perfectly aware there's no way this development could've escaped Diane's notice. Right now, I'd give half of what I'm worth for everyone around us to be temporarily relocated to a parallel universe so I can do what I'm dying to do. Cup her breasts. Fondle them. Pinch her nipples gently between my index and thumb. Slip my hand into her panties and stroke her until she pants. And then stroke her more until she writhes and moans. All the way to her orgasm.

*God, this isn't helping.*

I must stop thinking these thoughts at once. What I should do is glance at my phone, look concerned, and say I have to go.

Diane shifts in my lap as she leans forward, peering at the screen.

*Jesus. Christ.*

My lids drop, and I forget what I intended to do. My breathing becomes shallow. All I can think of is my hand in her panties.

*Would she be wet for me?*

"My money's on yes," Jeanne says.

I open my eyes. *What the fuck?*

Jeanne passes a napkin with a two-column table drawn on it to Manon. Manon scribbles something in the first column and hands the napkin to Elorie.

"What's that?" I ask Diane.

She looks over her shoulder. "We're betting on the Greek contestant."

She points to the screen where a guy in a shiny white suit is wailing yet another heartrending ballad while playing a grand piano.

"And?"

"In roughly fifty percent of performances that feature a piano—especially when the contestant is playing it himself—the instrument is set on fire at the end of the song." She smiles. "So the bet is if the Greeks will burn their piano."

"I see."

I feel a little stupid for having panicked a few seconds ago.

"What's your bet—yes or no?" Diane asks, holding the napkin.

"No," I say.

She puts my name in the second column and hers in the first.

A minute later, the piano burns.

I hand Jeanne a fifty euro bill and a two euro coin. "I have to go now."

She starts to rummage through the pocket of her apron.

"Keep the change," I say. "Please."

"OK. Thanks!"

Diane stands up.

"Please stay," I say to her. "I don't want to be a spoilsport."

She shakes her head. "You aren't."

We stare into each other's eyes, and I'm sure she's asking herself the same question I am—are we going to have sex tonight?

We say good-bye to Diane's friends and get into my car.

"You know," she says, "I still don't understand why you hired me knowing I had a chip on my shoulder."

I hesitate. "I have a confession to make."

"Go on."

"Part of the reason I picked you was guilt. I'm not proud of what I did to Charles, and I guess I wanted to buy myself a good conscience by supporting him through you."

"I don't get it. Isn't driving competitors out of business what you do all the time, what all successful businessmen do as you keep telling me. Why the sudden guilt?"

"I may have gone further with Charles than I usually do."

"Explain."

"I had my R and D team clone his bestsellers." I pause, hesitating again.

The corners of her mouth drop. "And then?"

"My sales team pushed them at half of his price." I glance at her. "He didn't have a chance."

For the next fifteen minutes, Diane fidgets with the three-carat rock on her ring finger as if itching to take it off. She won't talk to me.

It doesn't look like we'll be having sex tonight, after all.

And that's a good thing, right?

# Part IV
# Town House

# SEVENTEEN

I'm staring at the prints of my rooftop photos spread out on the floor of my TV room. Only half of them—that is, twelve out of twenty-four—will be on display at *La Bohème* starting next Monday.

The question is which twelve. And I'll be damned if I have a clue.

Earlier this afternoon, Chloe stopped by to help me choose. She left an hour later, utterly frustrated with my inability to make up my mind.

"They aren't your babies," she said with her hand on the doorknob. "They're just photos."

I made a face. "I know."

"And they're all great, anyway."

Does she realize how totally counterproductive her last comment was?

I go over the prints again, remembering the exact location, circumstances, and weather conditions of each shoot. Some of them are colorful and happy, like the ones I took in Buttes Chaumont. Others are black and white and melancholy, just like Paris feels sometimes when it's drowning in smog and drizzle. I can handle that sort of weather all right for twenty-four hours. After forty-eight hours, my mind begins to crave a respite. After seventy-two hours, my body starts to zombify. After a week of fog, the only solution to avoid a total collapse is an immediate southbound evacuation of my person.

This photo was taken atop Notre Dame—the only spot in Paris with a view of the seven bridges across the Seine—in the middle of an epic downpour. And this one I shot by night in late December, from the top of the Arc de Triomphe. I wasn't allowed to take my tripod up there, so I had to get creative. But, man, it was worth it! I took my best night shot of the Champs-Elysées with its horse chestnut trees wrapped in sparkling garlands, snowflakes dancing in the air, and an unobstructed view of the boulevard all the way to Le Louvre.

Chloe has a point—in some ways, my photos *are* my babies.

Ask a mother of two to pick the child she likes better, and you'll know what I'm going through. Besides, now that I've resigned from the supermarket, as per my contract with Darcy, I have a lot more time for photography. This is great, but it has a flip side. I spend even longer on editorial decisions than before.

My doorbell rings.

I startle and glance at the clock on the wall. It's seven in the evening—too early for Darcy. Elorie is still at work. Chloe must be on her way to Montrouge to see the house she and Hugo will be refurbishing next. And, anyway, none of these people ever show up on my doorstep without calling first.

Turns out one of them does after all—Darcy.

"You don't have to let me in if you don't feel like it," he says from behind the door. "I realize I should've called or buzzed from downstairs." He doesn't sound quite like himself.

"It's OK," I say, deciding that my tee and leggings are presentable enough, and open the door.

He steps in, holding a gorgeous bouquet in one hand and a bottle of vodka in the other.

I put my hands on my hips.

"I bought these from the florist two blocks down the street," he says, handing me the flowers.

"What's the occasion?"

He shrugs. "Can a man give his fiancée flowers without needing an occasion?"

He's definitely acting weird.

I cock my head. "Is the man in question drunk?"

"Just a little."

Darcy smiles his crooked smile, provoking a mild quake in my knees.

*I hate it when he does that.*

"Have a seat." I motion him to the couch in the TV room. "Oh, and if you step on any of the prints on the floor, I'll strangle you with your own overpriced tie."

"Understood." He makes his way to the couch, slaloming between the prints.

I set the flowers in the vase that Chloe left behind when she moved out and fetch a bottle of Orangina and two glasses from the kitchen.

He points at the vodka. "We should drink this first. The Poles swore it's the best vodka in the world."

"Which Poles?"

"From Mleko, the biggest milk product company in eastern Europe. They're market leaders for yogurt and ice cream in over a dozen countries. My deputy and I, and most of my legal team, have been working on this since February. As of today, Parfums d'Arcy is Mleko's main flavor supplier. We signed a deal this afternoon."

I arch an eyebrow "While eating yogurts and washing them down with Polish vodka?"

"Exactly," he says. "And with French champagne. And without the yogurts."

I shake my head in disapproval. "So, you down a few shots and decide that now is a good time to go check on Diane."

He spreads his arms. "The alternative was spending the rest of the evening carousing with my new partners. I told them it was my fiancée's birthday today."

"And left the poor Poles to carouse in a foreign city all by themselves?" I tut-tut.

"My deputy's with them, bless his heart." He opens the vodka and pours a little in each glass. "It's called Zubrowka, and it's flavored with bison grass."

I sigh.

"Come on, *chérie*," he says. "Don't be a spoilsport. I want you to tell me if Zubrowka is the best vodka you've ever had."

"I've only tasted one other vodka before. A Swedish one, I think."

"Must've been Absolut. It's owned by Pernod Ricard now." He hands me a glass. "You'll tell me how it compares to Absolut."

I take a sip, keep the liquid in my mouth for a moment, and swallow.

"Can you feel the woodruff and almond notes on the nose?" Darcy leans in. "And the vanilla near the end?"

"Err… I'm not sure."

He drinks the content of his glass. "Definitely vanilla at the end."

I empty mine. "It does have a sweet aftertaste... I guess."

"Have you eaten yet?"

"Uh-huh. You?"

He nods. "The Poles came with pickles and sausage to go with the vodka."

He refills our glasses. "Try to drink this like a Pole, *to the bottom*."

I nod and we both empty our glasses in one gulp.

"Are these the photos that'll be displayed at *La Bohème*?" Darcy asks, pointing to the floor.

"I have to discard half of them." I give him a mournful look. "It's killing me."

He squats in the middle of my prints and spends a few moments studying them.

"You really can't choose?"

"Nope."

He picks up the photo I took from the terrace of l'Institut du Monde Arabe and sets it on his left. "Yes."

Next, he takes a pic from the series I shot in the 11th. "No."

He continues, taking one pic after the other and sorting them into his yes and no piles. I watch him until he grabs my Latin Quarter roofscape and places it with the rejects.

Crouching next to him, I lift the photo and transfer it to the "yes" pile.

He smiles. "Ah, so you do have some favorites?"

"I don't. It's just… I almost broke my neck taking this one. If you leave it out, it's as if my almost sacrifice was for nothing."

"I don't like the sound of this." Darcy frowns. "Where exactly did you go to take these pictures?"

"All kinds of places." I hesitate before admitting. "Rooftops, mostly."

His frown deepens. "Do you actually *walk* on roofs?"

"I don't when it can be helped. But, you see, my camera… it's a solid Nikon, perfect for portraits, but it doesn't have a full-frame sensor, so it's not ideal for landscape photography."

"Why don't you buy another one?"

I raise my eyes skyward and sigh. *Rich people.* "Anyway, the way around it is to take multiple shots and combine them in Photoshop. It just requires that I move around the roof a bit."

He stares at me for a moment and nods. "OK, your Latin Quarter's in."

"*Merci, monsieur.*" I put my hand to my heart. "You're very kind."

Thirty seconds later, he's done.

I look at the two piles and then at him. "May I know what criteria you used in your super-efficient selection process?"

"None." He screws up his face in a way that's so sexy I nearly drool. "When pros and cons are in a tie, the only way forward is to shuffle them together, push them aside, and let your gut guide your hand."

"Is that what you just did?"

He nods. "But I can see why you were having such a hard time. They're all amazing."

"They better be." I smirk. "Considering that the photo lab's bill has put me in the red."

"Oh. I'm sorry to hear that."

I shrug. "The irony of it is that I could make better prints if I had the right equipment. And they'd be cheaper to produce."

"Really?"

"Oh, yeah."

"Wouldn't it be smarter to invest in the equipment instead of paying a lab to print your photos?"

"Sure," I say. "It would be much smarter."

"Then why—" He stops himself. "The cost. Listen, why don't I advance some of your fee so you can buy yourself a nice printer and a camera that's good for landscapes?"

I shake my head. "Your money goes to Dad. He'll need all of it to start over."

"In that case, I'd like to lend you some—"

"Thanks," I cut him off, "but no, thanks. I've managed fine so far with what I have, and I intend to go on until I save enough to afford what I want. There's no emergency."

He sucks his teeth, probably trying to come up with a counterargument.

"Hey, here's something you could do for me," I say to change the topic. "If you have any more tips on fast decision-making, I'll take them. I'm hopeless in that area."

His expression brightens. "It's certainly something you can improve with practice."

I set the photo piles on the coffee table and motion him to the couch.

"The first thing you can do," he says, "is narrow your field. In other words, discard all the options that aren't the best."

"OK. And then?"

"Remind yourself there's no perfect option, and that what you need is a decision that is fast and *roughly* right. That usually unblocks your gut instinct."

"Makes sense." I eye him up and down. "Have you always been so… decisive?"

He smirks. "No."

I wait for him to continue.

Instead he pours us two more vodka shots and raises his glass. "*Na zdrowie.*"

"Huh?"

"It means 'to your health' in Polish."

"*To the bottom?*" I ask.

He nods and empties his glass.

I do the same.

"Papa overdosed when I was twenty-three," he says. "I was *so* not prepared to fill his shoes. They seemed huge at the time…"

"Wasn't there someone else to run things for a while? A deputy or some experienced CEO?"

"We're a family business, and Papa had made sure it would be me who'd take charge if something happened to him."

"Did you *want* to take charge?"

He lets out a long breath. "In theory, yes. In practice, I wasn't ready. It's one thing to tell yourself that your future is in your hands. But realizing that the future of my younger brothers was in my hands, too—that came as a bit of a shock."

"How old were they?"

"Raph was nineteen and Noah only fifteen." He loosens his tie. "Do you mind if I remove this *overpriced* item?"

"Please."

He hangs it over the armrest and shrugs off his suit jacket. "My brothers had their trust funds, of course, and Maman was well taken care of, but most of the d'Arcy fortune was invested in the company."

"I see."

"Then I realized something else and it was even harder to stomach."

I give him a quizzical look.

"The livelihoods of hundreds of people employed by Parfums d'Arcy depended on me... When that realization hit me, it felt as if someone had loaded me up with a supersize backpack filled with rocks."

"How did you deal with it?"

"I created a persona." His lips curl. "I started acting as if I was the man Papa wanted me to be. Decisive. Unwavering. Someone who knows what he's doing."

"A real *homme d'affaires*."

He nods. "A man no one would dare call a greenhorn. A man his subordinates looked up to. I couldn't afford to show any sign of weakness or nonchalance." He smiles. "Not that I ever had any nonchalance to start with—that's Raphael's specialty."

"When my dad's business was going well," I say, "he hired someone to help him. It broke his heart when he had to let that person go a few years back. I can't imagine how it feels to know that hundreds of jobs hinge on your knowing what you're doing. That kind of responsibility would probably paralyze me into total inaction."

He leans toward me. "Let me tell you a secret. That's exactly how I felt, too, in the beginning. But I had no choice, so I began to… fake it. And I've been at it ever since."

"No way."

He nods and smiles. "I make my best guess and act on it with enough aplomb to convince everyone I *know* what I'm doing."

My head begins to turn as his charisma—yes, dammit, *charisma*—envelops me in a soft, yummy-smelling cocoon and lifts me up. The sentinels I've stationed throughout my brain sway on their feet and fall one after the other, clutching their mortal wounds.

It's a bloodbath.

With my first line of defense decimated, I can't help inhaling the heady scent coming off Darcy. I have no clue what part of it is *him* and what part is cologne, but the mixture does nasty things to me on some primal, subatomic level. He's a fragrance man, I remind myself. He must've had his labs concoct a highly potent love potion for his personal use.

*Hang in there, Diane!*

The question is, onto what? The impenetrable Anti-Darcy Defense Shield around my heart is melting away faster than I can regenerate it.

That is, if I could be bothered to regenerate it right now.

In a last-ditch attempt to avoid inglorious defeat and capitulation, I peel my gaze away from his darkened eyes. Only instead of focusing on the wall or the ceiling, my traitorous peepers zoom in on the bulge in his pants.

And what a nice, *voluminous* bulge it is!

On a rugged breath, I dig my fingers into my thighs and force myself to look away.

*Is it time to wave the white flag?*

Darcy takes my hand and covers it with his large palm.

I stare at his hands holding mine and then plunge into his bottomless gaze.

Resistance is futile.

I'm done for.

# EIGHTEEN

"You never told me what you did with the portraits of me you took at the castle," Darcy says, stroking my hand.

"I sold them to *Voilà Paris* for five hundred euros." I give him a saucy smile. "Would you like a share?"

"What will *Voilà Paris* do with them?"

"They'll use them at their discretion to illustrate various articles in future issues."

"Including the nude ones?"

I nod. "But don't worry, no one will know it's you in any of the pics. I made sure of it."

"I'm relieved." He looks at me with a mischievous gleam in his eyes. "You asked if I wanted a share."

"I give Elorie fifty percent for her nudes, so it's only fair I offer you the same rate."

"How about you pay me in kind instead?"

My heart skips a beat. "What do you have in mind, Sebastian?"

"I want to take a photo of you naked." His gaze burns into mine.

*Wow.*

What happened to his aristocratic stuffiness? Has all that Zubrowka gone to his unaccustomed Scotch-lover's head?

Good thing it hasn't gone to mine yet. What I'm going to do is laugh in his face and say he can shove his brilliant idea where the sun never shines.

I really should do that.

*Now.*

"Why?" I ask instead. "Are you planning to sell it to a men's magazine?"

"Of course not." He hesitates. "I'll keep it for personal use."

*Mmm.* My subservient mind generates an image of him reclining on his pillow in the privacy of his town house bedroom. He's holding a sexy nude photo of me in one hand while his other hand slides under the blanket. His gaze is dark and deep—just as it is now.

"OK," I say. "But only one shot, facing away."

He nods, looking as if he just up and made another billion.

I fetch my camera, moving fast, determined to get it into his hands before I change my mind. Sitting next to him, I screw on the lens, adjust the settings, and show him the basic functions.

"Take your clothes off, please," he says.

I lift my T-shirt over my head.

"Now the bra."

I undo the front clasp, spread the cups apart and flash my tits.

He leers like a starving wolf.

I grin, satisfied with the effect, and remove the bra completely.

"Now take off the bottoms."

My stomach flips as I stand. Just as my hands slide to the waistband of my leggings, a bulb goes on in my head. This is not how it's done. I signed up to pose for him—not to strip for him. The deal was that he takes a nude photo. He was supposed to turn away while I undressed.

That's how it's done.

*Fuck that.*

I hook my thumbs under the elastic band and peel my leggings down. There's no denying how much I'm enjoying doing this shoot the wrong way.

"The panties," Darcy rasps. He isn't even trying to pretend this is about the photo anymore.

I shake my head.

He raises an eyebrow. "No?"

"Not until you lift the camera."

For a moment, he looks as if he has no idea what I'm talking about before his gaze lands on the device in his hands. "Oh."

He raises the camera in front of his face, and I let out a little sigh of relief.

"Will you take your panties off now?" he asks, still seated.

I turn around, push the lacy thing down my hips and wiggle until it hits the floor.

"Step out of it," Darcy says.

I do.

"Go to the wall."

I obey.

"Place your hands on it and spread your legs apart."

Done.

"Now lift your hands… higher… lean forward."

As I do what he's asking… er, *ordering* me to do, I realize he's repeating my instructions from the castle shoot almost word for word. The difference is that I'm sent to the wall, while he was directed to the window. And that he's forgotten about the camera again.

I can't help smiling.

"Bend down," Darcy says.

Oh. Monsieur is *improvising* now.

"Is that really necessary?" I ask.

"Yes, it is," he says. "It's *very* necessary."

I turn my head to look into his eyes, and suddenly I'm not smiling anymore. The desire in his eyes hits me like a shockwave, so hard I nearly stagger.

"Bend down," he repeats, his eyes drilling into mine. "Please."

I turn back to the wall and lower my upper body until my breasts touch the cold wall and my backside sticks out in the most shameless way imaginable. Arousal and discomfort wrestle inside me. My ears are open for the click of the camera—the single shot I promised Darcy—after which I'll straighten up and march out of the room.

But that click never comes.

Instead, I hear Darcy put the camera down and lurch toward me. He grabs my wrists, shackling them to the wall, pushing me up, and leaning both of us into its hard surface. His large body presses against mine. He trails his mouth along the side of my face, chest squeezing against my back, groin nestled against my backside.

It's as if he's trying to get as close to me as humanly possible.

His free hand fondles my breasts, slides down, and lingers on my tummy. Heat pools in my pelvis in anticipation of its next stop. But instead of going further down, he glides it over my hips to my derriere. Darcy caresses it with the flat of his hand, softly at first and then in a more demanding manner, digging his fingers into my flesh.

I arch my back with the pleasure of it.

When his hand travels over my hips again, back to the front and down, I'm so ready it's ridiculous. The second his fingers ascertain that fact, a guttural growl rises from his throat.

He bends his head to my ear. "I want you, Diane. I want you so much."

These are trivial, overused words that millions of men have said to millions of women in the past. A few men have said them to me in the past. They're nothing to write home about. They shouldn't impress me. My knees shouldn't wobble in response. I shouldn't have to press my lips together so that my mouth doesn't plead, *Yes, please, take me, any way you want, just do it now!*

Instead, I reach behind my back to palm him through his pants.

He moans and drops hot, toothy kisses to my neck and shoulders as I rub. Then he steps back. I hear the click of a belt being unbuckled, the crisp sound of a zipper, and a foil tearing. Had he planned for this to happen, or does he always have a condom on him? He steps closer, slides his knee between my legs and nudges them wider apart.

I stand on tiptoes to make his entry easier.

He wraps an arm around me and plunges in.

The sweetness of it almost unbearable.

My head falls back into the crook of his neck. I inhale him—that unique, masculine scent that's so quintessentially Sebastian I can't imagine him smelling any other way.

He stirs inside me.

I roll my hips to encourage him.

"Diane," he groans and begins to thrust, alternating sharp lunges with gentler strokes.

When his cadence picks up and we find a rhythm that's just perfect, I lean back into his torso and let go of the last shreds of restraint. My legs start to shake, and I find myself moaning and saying his name.

"Diane... come for me," he grates between his thrusts.

My inner muscles contract around him a few seconds later.

And as they do, long and hard, muddled words erupt from me that are half plea, half order. "Yes, Sebastian, don't stop. Oh God, please, don't stop. Don't you dare stop!"

# NINETEEN

A question has been eating at me since I woke up ten minutes ago and found my bearings—Diane's bed, her apartment, late Saturday morning. Following a short night. Short because we spent most of it fucking in the living room, in the hallway, and here in this bed.

I barely noticed that question when it arose as I was thinking of something else. But, for some reason, it stuck in my mind. It blitzed out all my morning routines and is now invading the areas of my brain normally reserved for strategic thinking and processing of financial data.

Diane stands by the window, gazing outside, completely oblivious to my turmoil. She's wearing my shirt in lieu of a dressing gown. I was still asleep when she got up and put in on.

This burning question is killing me. All my neurons are currently working on it, desperate to figure out the answer before it's too late. I wouldn't go so far as to say my life depends on it, but my emotional and physical well-being certainly do. Perhaps even my sanity.

What I'm so desperate to know is whether Diane is *commando* under my shirt.

I can discern her nipples, so I know she didn't put on her bra. But the cotton of my shirt is too opaque to see through. What's worse, its weave is too tight to permit an educated guess regarding the presence of panty lines across her butt cheeks. If only she would bend down to pick something up, it would give me a fighting chance. But as things stand, my guesswork is perfectly ineffectual, and I'm scorching my neurons for nothing.

Would it be too rude to dig into the heap of our clothes on the floor and hunt for evidence? Last night, we undressed in the living room, so she must've fetched our clothes when she woke up. I could always pretend I'm looking for my own underwear. Except my boxers are in full view on top of that heap.

*Damn.*

Will she tell me if I ask her politely? Will she be sympathetic if I beg her to put me out of my misery? Or I should try a different tack and I announce that I need my shirt back? Will she take it off?

One thing is certain: If I do nothing, she's going to pick up her clothes and head to the bathroom. That will mean I'll *never* know. And I'll have to live with that glaring gap in my knowledge for the rest of my life.

"Last night was a mistake," Diane says without looking at me just as I'm about to stand up and do something radical such as slip my hands under the hem of that stupid shirt and get my answer.

It takes me a few moments to process her meaning. "I had the impression you enjoyed yourself."

She still won't turn toward me, but I can see her ears and cheeks color.

Good.

"I did," she finally says. "And that's the problem."

"Why?"

She spins around. "We're in a fake relationship that's soon to become a fake marriage. That's hard enough to handle. But if we start having sex…"

My thoughts exactly.

*Until last night.*

"Won't it be easier?" I sit up and stare into her eyes. "It'll actually make our fake love look more natural."

"I can't." She shakes her head. "It'll be too fucked up, even for me."

I think I know what the *real* issue is here. "You're afraid you'll fall in love."

"With you?" Her face contorts into a grimace. "You're the last man in the world I could ever fall in love with."

The vehemence of her denial would've been suspicious if the horror on her face were less sincere. I know Diane well enough by now to conclude she's truly appalled at the notion of falling in love with me.

That rattles my ego somewhat.

But I remind myself that I, too, would find the prospect of falling in love with her unpalatable. Diane is a radical leftist and an undereducated *have-not*. When I identified and hired her, she was lower in the societal food chain than most every person in my employ. Her father tried to elevate his family to a better life. But he failed due to poor business skills.

And yes, I'm aware that part of the reason he failed was me—the highborn *have* who crushed him like an annoying bug. And who believes that the best social order is when the elites are at the helm and the masses are at the oars.

"Excellent," I say. "I have no intention of falling in love with you, either. But I don't see why we can't have some fun while we're contractually bound to each other."

"My mind is made up." Diane gives me a hard stare. "I don't want this to happen again, and you have to respect that."

"Of course." I nod. "Not a problem."

An image of her face, flushed with arousal and pleasure as I stroke her core, pops into my head. Then another image of her moaning as I push into her. Ah, the sweetness of being inside her! I'm not prepared to give that up just yet. The desire will get stale, as it usually does, in just a few weeks. As for feelings, I'm perfectly safe from them. Even with Ingrid, whom I intended to marry, I never experienced that all-consuming emotion they call love. By the time my contract with Diane expires, I'll surely be through with her.

*But not yet.*

At this point in time, I want more of her sweet body, her pretty face and even her sharp tongue. She arouses me as much as she entertains me. And I know I arouse her as much as I repulse her.

Anyway, arguing now is pointless. She says she doesn't want to have sex with me again. Fine. So be it. I'm not going to beg her. Instead, I'm going to lie low and wait. Starting next Saturday and for the rest of the summer, Diane will live under my roof and sleep in my bedroom.

Who knows what will happen?

"When I move in with you," Diane says as if reading my mind, "do I absolutely have to share your bedroom?"

"It's in the contract."

"I know that. It's just… If I sneak out and sleep next door, no one will know." She gives me a pleading look.

"Let me ask you something. Have you ever slept in a house with live-in help?"

She shakes her head.

I sigh. "I thought so."

She smirks, and I realize my remark sounded more arrogant than I'd intended. But hey, Diane considers me an arrogant ass anyway, so I guess I'm just living up to her expectations. Anyway, I was trying to make a point.

"You see," I say. "You can fool your family—parents, children, siblings, cousins, grandparents... Grandmas can be perceptive, but even they can be duped. Who you can't fool is the people who serve you breakfast in the morning, make your bed, and clean your bathroom. They know everything."

"Do they?"

"Trust me, they do."

She turns away and stares out the window.

I'm sure she understands, but I want to make myself crystal clear.

"In addition to me," I say, "there are five other people living in my town house. Some of them you've met already, others you will the day you move in."

Diane gives me a sidelong glance, her expression wary.

"If we don't sleep in the same room," I say, "they'll know. I can't risk that."

"OK," she says. "Not a problem."

The next second, she picks up my boxers from the top of the pile and sets them on the bed. I watch, forgetting to breathe. She pulls my jeans from the bottom of the pile and places them next to my boxers. Then she grabs the rest of the pile, without sorting it, and heads to the bathroom.

"Sorry I borrowed your shirt," she calls from the hallway. "It won't happen again."

# TWENTY

The *majordome* opens the door and bows his head. "Welcome to Darcy House, mademoiselle. Everyone is thrilled about your arrival."

"Thank you, Octave." I clench my fists to stop myself from giving him a hug and a cheek kiss. "I'm thrilled to be here."

On my first couple of visits, I cheek kissed him. Then Darcy explained to me it was inappropriate and it made them uncomfortable. So, I've learned to keep my body language in check, hoping that my friendliness shows in the smile and the tone of my voice.

And that's how I greet the rest of the inhabitants of the mansion on rue Vieille du Temple—Lynette, a dynamic woman in her late fifties who helps Octave run the house; Michel, the cook with a proud beer belly that he calls his professional deformation; the shy maid, Lou; and Samir, the smiley gardener/handyman.

Samir carries my suitcases inside.

"Mademoiselle. Monsieur." Lynette hands Darcy and me a glass of bubbly. "This calls for a celebration."

Darcy touches his glass to mine. "It certainly does. Welcome to your future home, my dear."

I produce a saccharine smile. Someone, give me a *Légion d'Honneur* medal for not rolling my eyes.

We spend a few minutes in the foyer, sipping champagne and chatting with the staff. I insist that they call me by my first name. Lynette, Michel, and Samir promise they will. Octave says he can't. He'll call me *mademoiselle* and, once Darcy and I are married, he'll switch to *madame*. He apologizes profusely for his refusal to comply with my request, but he's just old-fashioned like that. It can't be helped.

When our glasses are empty and Lynette carries them away, Darcy takes my hand. "Let me show you around properly."

As we tour the airy *hôtel particulier*, Darcy explains that it was built almost four hundred years ago for a royal paramour. It changed hands many times and fell into disrepair in the nineteenth century when the aristocracy abandoned Le Marais. But his smart grandfather Bernard bought the mansion from a Swiss couple in the sixties, just before the neighborhood became hip again, and had it restored to combine the original grandeur with modern comforts.

"Have you always lived here?" I ask.

We've finished the tour, had a light dinner, and are now lounging in wicker armchairs in the most secluded and romantic spot in Darcy's picture-perfect back garden. The air is filled with the incomparable sweetness of a summer evening, enhanced by the climbing roses that lace the vintage cast-iron gazebo we're chilling in.

*Top marks, Samir!*

Darcy smiles.

I forget all about the roses.

Dammit, he's becoming an ace at this formerly so un-Darcy-like facial expression. Must be thanks to all the practice he's been getting lately, to my utter dismay. I'm determined not to slip again. Darcy hasn't made any intentional attempts to derail me— I'll grant him that. But he's been in the best of moods all week, laughing at my witticisms and even attempting a few of his own.

*Imagine that!*

He stopped by *La Bohème* every night—just as I did—to watch customers look at my photos, and he celebrated with me every print I sold.

The problem is Darcy being sweet, supportive, and funny is just as bad as deliberate seduction. No, it's worse. Much worse.

Give me the biblical serpent and his juicy apple any day over this.

"Yes," he says. "I've lived in this house since I was born, with a hiatus of five years in my late teens and early twenties."

"Don't tell me you lived in a student dormitory during your *hiatus*."

He shakes his head. "But I assure you, my accommodations were modest."

"What made you return home?"

"It's a long story."

I stretch out my legs, cross my ankles, and lift the glass of homemade lemonade in my hand. "Do I look like I'm in a hurry?"

"OK," Darcy says after a short hesitation. "I moved back here sometime after Maman left and before Papa passed."

He sips his lemonade in silence, his expression somber. Whatever thoughts he's thinking aren't happy.

Darcy sets his glass on the metal table and turns to me. "Both of my parents entered a delayed and severe midlife crisis when I was about nineteen. Papa turned into a compulsive *bon vivant*. When he wasn't gambling in Monaco, he sailed in the Mediterranean or raced his Lamborghini around Tuscany. He'd come home only to see his boys and then be off again on his next adventure."

"You and your brothers lived with your dad?"

He shakes his head. "I was renting an apartment in the 6th, and my brothers lived with Maman."

"Who ran the company?"

"No one, really. It kind of ran itself—those were the good old days before the subprime mortgage crisis. Only at some point, the company started running *downhill*."

"What about your mom?"

He sighs. "Papa tried really hard to win her back and persuade her to join him on his fun-in-the-sun trips, but she despised all of it. Her own midlife crisis led her in the opposite direction."

"To the North Pole?"

He snorts. "Maman became very religious and passionate about charity work."

"If you were nineteen, your brothers were…" I close my eyes, computing.

"Raphael was about fifteen and Noah eleven." A shadow passes over his face. "They needed their parents. An older brother, a butler, tutors, cooks, maids, and extravagant amounts of pocket money can't stand in for mom and dad."

"I guess not."

"One day I stopped by the house and caught Raph smoking pot with a couple of other kids like him." Darcy's lips compress into a hard line. "With too much money and too little supervision."

"Did you tell your parents?"

He shakes his head. "There was no point. Papa would've freaked out and overreacted, and Maman... let's just say we weren't close."

"What did you do?"

"I took measures." He shrugs. "Someone had to."

"Did your measures work?"

"Oh, yeah." He gives me a smug smile. "And I didn't stop there. Someone also had to convince the company's employees and the staff here and in Burgundy that the d'Arcys weren't on a path to self-destruction."

"But you were only nineteen!"

"It's not as if we had other candidates for the task." He chews on his lip. "Besides, I was already twenty-one by the time Papa involved me in the business."

It's funny how his voice, tone, and eyes are neutral when he says *Maman* and filled with warmth when he says *Papa*.

"You loved him, didn't you?" I ask.

He smiles. "Papa was the best. A great guy—kind, generous, incredibly charismatic—despite his poor judgement and mistakes. Yes, I loved him, even when he went through his personality yo-yo... I loved him more than I've ever loved anyone."

That's how I feel about my dad, too.

I tuck a strand of hair behind my ear. "You wanted to help him any way you could, didn't you?"

"Yes, I did. But, as it turned out, I couldn't save him from himself." He shrugs. "So I resolved to at least save his name and his life's work. His legacy."

"I thought you didn't care much for the family name." I wink at him. "You did shorten it to Darcy, after all."

"It's just to make the conduct of business easier. I didn't want to put a certain type of people off with my long name and my title."

*People like me?*

I narrow my eyes. "Fess up, Sebastian—you're actually proud to be Count d'Arcy and so forth, aren't you? You burn the midnight oil drawing your family's coat of arms and reading up about the lives and deeds of your illustrious ancestors all the way back to Charlemagne."

"We don't descend from Charlemagne. The first recorded d'Arcy du Grand-Thouars de Saint-Maurice was a knight of Irish descent ennobled in the sixteenth century."

He smiles.

Slowly, his smile stretches into a grin. A grin of the panty-dropping variety.

I focus on my lemonade.

"I suppose I *am* proud of my ancestry and *most* of their deeds," Darcy says. "That pride was one of the things that kept me going all those times I was a hair from saying screw it all."

I gaze at the white roses over my head. What I just heard explains a lot about Darcy. But not all. It doesn't explain why he had to be so hard on my dad. The man was no threat to him. Dad's artisanal workshop was a little mosquito to Darcy's King Kong.

Couldn't he just live and let live?

Why hadn't he at least attempted to buy Dad's fragrances before he "cloned" them and drove the man out of business?

I'll never forgive myself if I forgive him for what he did.

"Why exactly did your mom leave your dad?" Darcy asks out of the blue.

"I'm not sure I want to talk about it."

"I answered your questions," he says. "Now it's your turn."

"Fine."

"So?"

"Several reasons," I say. "His drinking, of course. Dad can't hold his liquor, and he'd sworn to quit when they got married. He kept his promise until... until you ruined him."

"I see."

"She tried to help him, she really did. She got a waitressing job and urged him to do the same."

"Wait tables?"

"Get a job. Move on." I shrug. "But he was stuck on saving his company—his baby—at any price. When Mom discovered he'd secretly taken a mortgage on the house, she went ballistic."

"I can imagine."

"He faked her signature!" I shake my head. "I think it was the last straw."

Darcy nods. "She couldn't forgive his lie."

"Not just that. She loves that house. They bought it shortly after they married, and completely rebuilt it over the years. It's where they raised Lionel, Chloe, and me. We still have our rooms there, always ready for an impromptu visit."

His gives me a sympathetic look. "She kept Lionel's room?"

"Yes." I rake my hand through my hair. "I used to tell her she should empty it out, but now I'm glad she never did. When I go in there, I remember him and my childhood… It's always bittersweet, but it's more sweet than bitter."

He reaches over and takes my hand. I tell myself it's just to say he's sorry for my loss. He's trying to convey that he, too, knows what it feels like to lose a dear one.

He'll let go of it in a moment.

Lynette comes out of the house, carrying a fragrant candle in an ancient chandelier. She sets it on the table between our armchairs.

I realize it's dark. A quick glance at my watch confirms the lateness of the hour—a quarter past eleven.

"I'm off to bed, children," she says, smiling. "Remember to blow out the candle when you go in."

"Will do," Darcy says.

He's still holding my hand.

I'm still deluding myself he'll release it any moment now.

Instead, he gives it a gentle squeeze and strokes the inside of my palm with his thumb.

Lynette's steps fade away and a door clicks shut.

Darcy tugs on my arm. "Come here."

In the candlelight, his eyes are two bottomless black wells, the pull from their depths almost irresistible.

I tip my head back and peer at the stars through the holes in the foliage. Dear Lord, I'm weak, so freaking weak. I'm about to let Darcy pull me toward him and have his way with me. My libido is taking control of my brain in a way I hadn't anticipated. My lust has become the enemy within—a traitor only too happy to do the rival power's bidding to the detriment of his homeland.

Darcy gives me another gentle tug, and I go to him, a slave to my baser needs. Without standing up, he leans toward me and runs his hands over my hips and thighs. He strokes them, down to my knees and up to my bottom, sliding his hands under the hem of my sundress.

I move closer and sit on his lap, facing him, my legs on either side of his. He nudges the straps of my dress and bra down my shoulders. Dying for the feel of his hands on my breasts, I pass my arms through the straps. The material slithers down and pools at my waist.

Sebastian reaches behind my back, unclasps my bra, and finally cups my breasts with his big hands. His touch is warm and snug and necessary.

*Wait a sec!*

Did I just call him "Sebastian"? Not because I had to, but of my own free will, inside my head where there are no witnesses?

Yes, I did.

This is *so* messed up.

I inch closer to his hard-on, debating if I should free it now or wait. When he puts his mouth to one of my breasts and begins to suckle, I forget what it was I couldn't make up my mind about. The softness of his lips, the tightness of his latch around my areola and the sweet intimacy of his tongue on my nipple make me arch and whimper.

He grips the back of my neck, raking his fingers through my hair, and pulls me to him. When his kiss arrives, openmouthed and hot, I revel in every exquisite moment of it, in his heady taste. It occurs to me that *extra hot* has become our new normal when we're alone. It also hits me that he no longer asks for permission to kiss me like that.

*Thank God.*

Who knew I'd love spice so much?

As we kiss, I begin to feel the ache and the emptiness in my core, exactly the way I did before our first time a week ago.

I hope he has protection because I really don't see how I can make it to the bedroom.

The urge to touch him overwhelms me. I undo his belt and zipper, draw his boxer-briefs down, and wrap my fingers around him.

He makes a noise deep in his throat and pulls a condom out of his pocket.

My famished body cheers and pops champagne.

"When we get to the bedroom," he says, sheathing himself, "I'm going to kiss and lick you absolutely everywhere."

"Including the toes?"

"Oh, yes."

I sigh theatrically. "Do your worst."

"Trust me, I will."

"If you're trying to impress me," I say, raising my chin in defiance, "it isn't working."

*It's working just fine—I'm soaking wet.*

He smiles. "I'm not trying to impress you. I'm just giving you a heads-up."

I zoom in on his erection, proud and unapologetic, like the rest of him. "What if I walked away now and left you hanging... er, getting it up?"

He stares at me. "You wouldn't."

"I could."

Gripping my hips, he pulls me close enough for our sexes to brush. "But you won't."

As he says those words, Sebastian tugs the crotch of my panties to the side and drives in.

*You're right—I won't.*

# TWENTY-ONE

"Another cappuccino?" Lynette asks.

I smile at her. "Thank you, but two is enough this early in the day."

Actually, it isn't *that* early.

The others have been up for at least a couple of hours. Three, in Sebastian's case. Lynette and I are the only late risers, so we've gotten into the habit of taking our breakfast together. Besides, everyone else favors the minimalistic French breakfast of coffee, orange juice, and croissant. Lynette and I like *real* breakfasts.

And real breakfasts require prep work.

So, it goes like this: Lynette makes pancakes or porridge, fries eggs, and brews coffee that's second only to Manon's. I pick and wash a handful of strawberries from the garden and then toast some bread. When everything's ready and we sit down, Lynette opens the paper Sebastian has left for her, and I check the newsfeed on my phone. Sometimes we chat, but mostly we just enjoy our big, fat, and infinitely rewarding breakfast in companionable silence.

I help Lynette clear the table and head upstairs.

Today Octave is out of town visiting his mother's grave and taking care of some private matters. I'll be using this opportunity to snoop around his quarters. He's Sebastian's most trusted staff member, so I figure maybe I'll find something.

But the moment I open the door to Octave's office, the knot in my stomach doubles in size, forcing me to stop and take a few fortifying breaths.

I inspect my palms.

Clean.

Funny, I would've bet they were smeared with sticky mud.

What I'm about to do feels so wrong I'm a hair from backpedaling. It's one thing to nose into Sebastian's life, but intruding on an innocent man's— a *good* man's—private space isn't something I can easily justify.

However, considering I still haven't found any dirt whatsoever on my betrothed, I have no choice.

How naive I was to imagine that once I lived here, I'd gain access to his financial information or the inner workings of his business! The documents he keeps in his home office are as innocuous as a document could be. He may as well publish them online. He never discusses sensitive matters with me or when I'm around. Or when anyone is around.

Sebastian's life is so perfectly and hermetically compartmentalized it should be used as a case study in management books.

When working, he's a steely business shark. In his private life, he's a loyal friend and brother, and a respected master of the house. He's also the most gallant of men with yours truly... on camera. At night, his alpha side comes out again, only in a different way. He forgets his good manners and becomes demanding and greedy.

It seems duplicity is his second nature.

As for me, I've taken a page from his book, forcing myself to compartmentalize, too.

I crave his brand of sex. I enjoy his conversation. I have a hard time keeping my eyes or hands off him.

All true, all undeniable.

But deep inside, I'm still the person who attacked him with a cream cake last October. I'm not impressed by his riches. Well, maybe just a little. It would take a saint not to be. And I'm no saint—not even close.

What Sebastian will never have is my forgiveness.

Even if I'm soon to become Madame d'Arcy du Grand-Thouars de Saint-Maurice, I'm still *me*. And I still care more about justice than I do about money.

On that thought, I force myself to step in and look around.

The first thing I notice is a black-and-white portrait of a smiling young woman on Octave's desk. Her hair is huge, its ends curled and flipped up, and she wears more eyeliner than Sophia Loren and Aimee Winehouse combined. The adorable portrait screams "the sixties" in all its rock 'n' roll glory.

This must be Octave's mom.

I note there's no portrait of his dad anywhere. From what I gather, the man is still alive, even if Octave never talks about him. Maybe they don't get along.

But I should stop distracting myself—it isn't Octave I'm after.

I spend the next hour going through the perfectly organized and labelled files on the wall shelves. They contain nothing but bills, contracts, bank statements, and administrative correspondence.

A roomy cabinet next to Octave's desk hosts an unusual-looking audio device and headphones. Maybe he's an amateur radio broadcaster or something in that vein.

Next up, his desk.

When I realize that some of the drawers are locked, I'm relieved. This means I'll get out of here sooner.

The guilt is killing me.

I open the unlocked ones. Pens, scissors, staplers, paper... One drawer contains Octave's passport and his birth certificate.

*Octave Bernard Rossi, born March 14, 1958.*

Ha! I didn't know his middle name was Bernard, like Sebastian's grandfather's. But let's face it, if my middle name was Bernard, I'd keep mum about it, too. It's undeservedly but irrevocably *démodé* and even mossier than Octave, which, at least, is original and even appears to be making a comeback.

As I close the last drawer and tiptoe out the door, I beg Heaven to forgive me this particular trespass.

And then I beg for a memory wipe so my tongue will never slip and call poor Octave by his unfortunate middle name.

# TWENTY-TWO

"Welcome back, madame." Octave performs his signature head bow and takes a suitcase from Sebastian. "Monsieur, it's good to see you smiling and tanned. I hope everything went as planned."

"Better than planned," Sebastian says, heading upstairs with the rest of our baggage. "It was a *perfect* wedding."

And in many ways, it was.

Now that I've faked a marriage to the man, I find it hard to believe it's been only a month since I moved in with him in mid-May. This has been the speediest month of my life. Almost every night, we've gone out or hosted a dinner at home. Sebastian has been acting as a man utterly and completely smitten with his fiancée. When I took him to Nîmes, he charmed the bejesus out of Mom and all my childhood friends.

I didn't dare to take him to Marseilles.

In fact, I didn't even have the courage to tell Dad about him. Chloe did that for me.

As expected, first he was shocked. And then he was mad.

I hope he'll forgive me one day after I've completed my mission and he's put two and two together.

If that day ever comes, that is.

Because so far, the muddiest, stinkiest dirt I've found on my fiancé is a speeding ticket.

Our wedding was an "intimate" affair, held in the privacy and extreme luxury of a paradisiac Bahamian island. My fiancé told everyone we couldn't wait for the chateau wedding scheduled for next May, to which everyone and their cat will be invited. This gave rise to rumors that I'm pregnant, which both of us denied so vehemently that a lot of people decided they were true.

The ceremony took place on a pristine sand beach with only the minister, Sebastian, a handful of guests, and me to stain its unspoiled purity. I wore a bespoke wedding dress of hand-embroidered silk and exquisite *Alençon* lace. It hugged my body like a glove, pushing my breasts up and flaring out at the hem.

Now that Sebastian and I are on shagging terms, wearing sacks is kind of pointless.

Our handpicked guest list included Raphael and his bestie Genevieve, Sebastian's aunt and uncle, and a few of his closest friends including Laurent, who arrived alone, and Mat, who came with Jeanne.

Sebastian's mother and his youngest brother Noah were "unable"—read "unwilling"—to attend.

My side consisted of Mom, Chloe and Hugo, two childhood friends from Nîmes, and Elorie. Manon couldn't make it.

Unsurprisingly, neither could Dad.

A couple of weeks before the wedding, Sebastian published the banns, which made me jittery.

"Are you sure our marriage is truly fake?" I asked him for the umpteenth time.

"Better than that," he said. "It's *genuinely* fake. Everything is real and legit, in case anyone wants to check."

Color drained from my face.

"Don't look so terrified!" He laughed. "I *forgot* to submit a crucial piece of paperwork to the closest French consulate in Miami. I'll be sure to keep forgetting for three more months, after which our marriage will be null."

I exhaled in relief.

"My dearest, Diane." He patted my hand. "I have just as little desire to marry you for real as you do. So relax and enjoy your fake wedding and honeymoon."

And so I did.

We both did, judging by my new husband's insatiable appetite throughout the week. We fooled around at the hotel, on the beach, up against a palm tree, in the sea, in the pool, in the Jacuzzi, in the shower, on the bed, on the couch, on the floor, and against the wall in our palatial suite.

Against every wall in our suite.

The whole week was a nonstop sexfest, leaving certain parts of my body a little sore, but also pleasured beyond my wildest fantasies.

On the way home, I sat next to Chloe for a good part of the endless flight. We talked about her physical and emotional recovery, and how she was beginning to see life in a different light. She said it felt like putting on Technicolor lenses after years of gray scale. Happiness still scares the shit out of her, but she's learned to breathe through her fear and carry on.

"I'm grateful for every day with Hugo," Chloe said, staring at the blue expanse above the clouds. "It took me a while to recognize that he's the love of my life. But now that I have…" She paused, her expression dreamy.

"What has changed, now that you have?" I asked.

"I keep falling in love." She smiled. "Every day, I tell myself it isn't possible to love a man more than I love Hugo, and yet the next day I find myself loving him more."

"Your fiancé is a wonderful man," I said.

And I meant it.

"And you"—Chloe gave me a wink—"still haven't told me how you went from hating Sebastian Darcy to marrying him six months later."

"It's a long story," I said, borrowing his favorite excuse.

Fortunately, Chloe didn't point out that we were stuck on a plane with nothing to do for a few more hours.

Good girl.

# TWENTY-THREE

Finally in the quiet and comfort of the master bedroom at Darcy House, I stretch out on the bed and catch a quick nap while Sebastian showers.

Lucky bastard—he had no problem sleeping on the plane.

"I'm off to the office," he says, emerging from the bathroom all crisp and kissworthy. "Lots of catching up to do."

"Go catch them all up, *darling*!" I produce a nauseatingly saccharine smile. "What's a little jet lag to a captain of industry?"

He laughs. "What about you?"

"Bath. Pajamas. Sleep."

"It's only four in the afternoon."

I give him a "so what" shrug.

As soon as Sebastian is gone, I take a long bath and put on my PJs. The problem is I can't sleep. With no industry to captain and no catching up to do, I should've dropped off the moment I shut my eyes. But my wayward brain has decided otherwise. After thirty minutes of vain attempts to cop some z's, I give up and get dressed.

Too tired to read, I decide to explore the last unchartered area of Darcy House—the attic. Vast and high-ceilinged, it's used for storage—an unpardonable waste of space in any *normal* person's point of view. As I climb the wooden staircase and step into the loft, I remember Sebastian telling me his father wanted to install an indoor swimming pool in here. But the city of Paris denied him the permit, what with the mansion being classified as a historic building.

Poor rich man, he must've been heartbroken!

I wander around, running my hand over mismatched pieces of furniture and unveiling old paintings stacked against the walls. Specks of dust dance in the light coming in through dormer windows. The place smells of old wood and the lavender hanging from the ceiling beams in little dried bunches. The attic has so much character and charm that if I were the *real* mistress of this house, I would've wiped the dust, washed the windows, and set up my workspace here.

But as things stand, I'm the *fake* mistress of this house, and my goal is to find dirt on my fake husband.

*Get to work, Diane.*

I begin with the massive chest of drawers in front of me and work my way through the loft, leaving no object unturned. Two hours later, just as I begin to tell myself this is pointless, I pull out the middle drawer of an unpretentious little desk that's hiding behind a gigantic throne-like armchair and stacks of old magazines.

Weird... The drawer looks shallower than its siblings.

Using my tiny Swiss army knife—Lionel drilled into me to always have it handy—I hook the false bottom of the drawer and lift.

*Bingo!*

Concealed underneath is a secret compartment that holds a bundle of four letters. I open the first one. It's from Sebastian's mom, accusing her ex-husband of having turned their older sons against her and insisting Raphael would be much better off living with her in Nepal than with him in Paris. Why only Raphael, I wonder before remembering that Noah was already with her and Sebastian must've been around twenty by then.

The second letter is more or less the same as the first with the addition of a few choice adjectives I wouldn't've expected from a high-society lady.

The third letter, again from her and again on the same topic, ends with this passage:

> *I was hoping it would never come to this, but your blatant refusal to meet me halfway leaves me no choice. So here goes. Do you remember how I was already pregnant with Sebastian when we married? I'm sure you do. What you don't know is that I wasn't pregnant by you. That's right—Sebastian, your adored firstborn, your rock and your heir, is not your son. He's Emmanuel's. If you don't believe me, you're welcome to steal a few hairs from Sebastian's comb and have them tested. Once you've done that, it's up to you to wait until I tell him the truth or to send Raphael to live with me.*
>
> *Marguerite*

I reread the passage twice more and then open the fourth—and last—letter and read the following:

*Thibaud,*

*I'm glad you did the paternity test. Now that you have proof that I wasn't bluffing, will you please send Raphael to me? I promise that if you do, I'll never tell Sebastian the truth. It would break his heart. But I'm prepared to do that if you leave me no choice. It is my duty to shelter Raphael, who lacks his older brother's sense of purpose and moral rectitude, from your debauched lifestyle. I hope you understand my motives and will do the right thing.*

*Marguerite*

The letter is dated a month before Darcy senior overdosed.

This revelation must've been the straw that broke his back. He'd already lost his wife, his good name, and his youngest son. He was being blackmailed and pressured to send his middle son to a faraway country. But, perhaps worst of all, he'd been robbed of his oldest and favorite boy. Not in the literal sense, but on that fundamental *fruit-of-my-loins* level, which means more to us than it should.

With shaking hands, I fold the letters and stick them in the back pocket of my jeans.

That's it.

My mission is accomplished. I've found the muddy, stinky dirt that I've been looking for.

The dirt that could destroy Sebastian Darcy.

# TWENTY-FOUR

The round-faced pastry shop assistant gives me a bright smile. "What can I get for you, mesdemoiselles?"

"A small bag of *coucougnettes*, please," I say politely.

Elorie snorts. "Did you just ask for testicles?"

"I did." I pay and offer a soft pink sweet from my bag to Elorie. "I promise you'll like it."

She studies the almond paste "ball" spiced with ginger and candied in sugar and pulls a face. "Really?"

I nod to encourage her. "They're a Southwest specialty, but I discovered them only a month ago here in Le Marais."

Elorie puts the *coucougnette* in her mouth and chews it slowly.

"So?" I ask.

"Tastes better than it sounds."

I grin. "Told ya."

We step out and amble along the cobblestone streets of this medieval *quartier* until our next stop—the European House of Photography. The exhibition space is located in an eighteenth-century *hôtel particulier* at 5 rue de Fourcy. Impressive as it is, the building can't hold a candle to the splendor of Darcy House.

It's just an impartial observation, that's all.

The plan is to split up for a while. While I check out the new exhibit at the photography museum, Elorie will explore the best vintage clothes shop in the capital just around the corner on rue de Rivoli.

An hour later, I leave the museum and head to the "falafel street"—rue des Rosiers. When I arrive, Elorie is already standing in the long line in front of L'As du Fallafel.

She holds up a big plastic bag filled with clothes. "Your new neighborhood rocks."

"I know!" I grin. "Where else in Paris can you have so much fun on a Sunday afternoon?"

"Unfortunately, being so cool has a flip side." She sighs and points at all the people ahead of us in line. "I hope you aren't too hungry."

"Fear not, my friend." I pull the *coucougnettes* bag from my purse and wave it in front of her nose. "We have balls."

Fifteen minutes later, the line has barely moved.

"You know," Elorie says, helping herself to a pink bonbon, "sometimes I hate this country."

"Why's that?"

"It's all about *égalité*, but when you scratch below the surface, there's no real equality. What we have is a sky-high fence between the rich and the poor."

"I agree," I say. "But I would argue it isn't as tall as it seems."

Elorie shakes her head. "Your Cinderella story, *ma cocotte*, is so improbable it's suspicious. A man like Sebastian Darcy falling in love with a cashier? Marrying her? You have to admit it sounds fishy."

Of course it does.

*Because it is.*

"Hey, what about your 'marry-a-billionaire' plan?" I ask. "If you don't believe in Cinderella stories, aren't you wasting your time plotting to snatch a prince?"

"Maybe I am." Elorie bites her nails, her expression morose. "I haven't had much success, even with all the opportunities you're throwing my way."

I give her hand a squeeze.

Suddenly, she perks up. "I know what I have to do! I need to adjust my strategy and focus on the *nouveau-riche* billionaires. The *new* money, not the old."

"Athletes? Start-up wonder kids?"

"Yes, but also mafia bosses." She shrugs. "They'll be less picky."

What can I say to that?

If anything, my fake Cinderella story only proves she's right.

Best to change the topic. "Remember I told you about Belle Auxbois and how she didn't want to credit Dad for his work?"

She nods.

"You won't believe it, but she changed her mind."

Elorie holds her thumbs up while chewing another *coucougnette*.

"Dad sent me a link to the talk show that aired on TF1 last Saturday."

Elorie widens her eyes. "She went on TV with it?"

"Yup." I beam. "Prime time. The show host asked her about the perfume, which is selling really well, and she said she hadn't done it alone. She admitted she'd had precious help from Charles Petit, one of the country's best *parfumiers*."

"She said that?"

"Uh-huh." I can't wipe the grin off my face. "Isn't it fantabulous? I have no idea what triggered her sudden confession, though. Maybe she just woke up one morning and realized that acknowledging Dad's work was the right thing to do."

At last, we enter the eatery. Just as I'm about to order a falafel plate with a side of grilled eggplant, Elorie claps her hand to her forehead. "I know why she caved in."

I stare at her expectantly.

"It's your husband."

"What?"

"When I stayed over at the castle, I overheard him talking on the phone with someone. He sounded stern, even a little scary."

"What did he say?"

"He mentioned the perfume, some other stuff I didn't understand, and said things like 'I have proof' and 'it's in your best interest to announce it yourself.' "

"Anything else?"

Elorie furrows her brow, trying to recall. "Oh yeah, he also said 'I'm giving you a month, and then I'm suing the pants off you.' "

I can't believe what I'm hearing. "Why didn't you say anything before?"

"I didn't make the connection." She gives me an apologetic shrug. "It's only now that everything clicked into place."

I can't think of much else for the rest of our girls' day about town.

We say good-bye at *République*, and I take the *métro* to my apartment in the 14th, which Sebastian has been paying for since I chucked the supermarket job.

My head throbs as I struggle to adjust to Elorie's revelation about Sebastian.

And to how I can possibly reconcile it with what I intend to do.

# TWENTY-FIVE

Two hours later, after I get to my apartment and frame the rest of my rooftop prints for Jeanne's gallery, my thoughts are still in a jumble of epic proportions.

So, Sebastian worked behind the scenes to help Dad, and hid it from me. Clearly, he didn't do it to improve my opinion of him. Does this mean he's sorry for what he's done to Dad? Is this his way of making amends?

Am I prepared to forgive him?

After all, he can truly be held responsible only for Dad's bankruptcy. My parents' divorce and Dad's stroke were the consequences of that but they weren't, strictly speaking, Sebastian's fault.

There's another question that's been growing in the back of my mind for weeks now. It started as a tiny seed that I could ignore, but it's exploded inside my head, deafening me.

*Could our fake relationship ever turn into something real?*

I lean my forehead against the window and stare outside.

*Don't be daft, woman.*

Sebastian and me, it'll never work. We're like fire and ice, matter and antimatter. We're wired for mutual destruction. Whatever it is that's sprouted between us, it's doomed.

I read *Libération*, vote for socialists, and believe in strong government. He gripes about France's "archaic" labor laws that "overprotect" employees and discourage entrepreneurial initiative. Even though in public he supports the Greens, I'm sure it's only because his PR people told him it's good for the company's image. Deep inside, he's as conservative as it gets.

He's a billionaire, for Christ's sake.

And he reads *Le Figaro*.

I hate that kind of people. They have no civic sense, no notion of solidarity. Their only concern is how to make more money and pay less in taxes. And while these glorified crooks succeed in dissimulating their income in Swiss banks and offshore companies, people like Dad—hardworking, honest people—go belly up.

I rack my brain for additional arguments.

What I'm trying to do here is to wind myself up into a righteous anger against Sebastian. Only a couple of months ago, I had no difficulty doing it.

It used to come naturally.

But now, all my valiant attempts hit a brick wall and fly into pieces. That wall is the belief—a conviction, really—that Sebastian is nothing like the rotten, self-absorbed golden boy that I've been painting him to be. His arrogance is superficial. It's just a mask he wears to hide his insecurities from the world. And to project an image of someone who "knows what he's doing."

Underneath the veneer, Sebastian Darcy is an honorable man in every single way that matters.

I take my head in my hands, wishing I was on a deserted island so I could bawl my confusion to the four winds.

My door buzzer sounds.

It's Sebastian.

I let him in, wondering what's so urgent it couldn't wait 'til I get to the town house later tonight.

He steps in, a huge cardboard box in his hands.

"What is this?" I ask as he sets it on my desk.

"A top-notch professional-quality printer," he says. "So you can make your own prints. And a landscape camera."

I sit down, flabbergasted.

He opens the box and unpacks the printer first. Unable to resist, I jump up and take a closer look. He's right—it's top-notch equipment. To think of all the stuff I could do with it…

"I hope this is what you were talking about." He hands me a camera.

Not just any camera—a Seitz 6x17 Panoramic.

I've read articles about it. I've dreamed about it. This baby takes the world's largest digital photos. The quality is so good I can make a wall-sized print of the Chateau d'Arcy and still be able to see the little spider swinging under one of the third-floor windows.

It's the best of the best of the best.

I push it back toward him. "This thing costs a small fortune. More than what I make in a year."

"It's nothing," he says.

"I can't accept it."

"And I can't have you walking on roofs so that you can take enough shots with your portrait camera to assemble them into a landscape."

"Why…" I look away, trying to form my question. "Why are you being so nice to me?"

"Do you want the conveniently honest answer or the brutally honest one?"

"Give me both."

He places the camera on the table, takes my chin between his index and thumb, and turns my face toward him.

I stare into his somber eyes.

"The conveniently honest answer is that I'm *nice* to you because I like your photos and want to help."

"And the brutally honest one?"

"I'm being *nice* because I want to continue seeing you after our contract expires and you *leave* me."

"You want a real relationship?"

"I'm not sure that's exactly what I'd call it." He hesitates. "Diane, I don't want to mislead you or give you false hopes. You're *not* the kind of woman I'd ever pick as a real wife."

I square my shoulders, trying not to show how much his words hurt me.

"You despise what I stand for," he says. "You have no interest in my world, in being my *partner* in every aspect of life." He pauses before adding, "My mother had the same distaste for the things that mattered to Papa... And look where it got them."

He lets go of my chin.

We're both silent for a long moment, gazing out the window, at our shoes, at the equipment on the table—everywhere except each other.

I'm the first to break the silence. "Thank you for your honesty."

His gaze burns into my eyes as he waits for me to continue.

"I think it would be best if we stopped seeing each other after the contract expires," I say.

His face hardens. "If that's what you want."

I nod.

*Dammit*, this conversation is hard.

"Tell me something," I say to get us out of the minefield. "Why are you so sure your nemesis will use the same method on you as he did on your father? Maybe this time he'll do something different, something more drastic."

"Like what?"

"I don't know… poison you?"

He laughs. "I don't think so."

"Why not?"

"It's just not his MO. You see, the guy—or the gal—hates me, but he won't take unnecessary risks. He's super careful."

"If you say so."

"From what I've observed, he seeks to inflict pain—not to kill. What he wants is to punch me where it hurts most. If I wither and die as a consequence, he probably won't complain. But his goal isn't my quick death. I'm sure of it."

*Punch me where it hurts most.*

Isn't that what I'll do to him if I make those letters public?

He doesn't need his nemesis to give him pain and suffering—he has me.

"Ready to go home?" he asks after our conversation returns to the equipment I've agreed to keep.

"You go ahead," I say. "I still have some stuff to do."

"Need help?"

I shake my head. "Need privacy."

He nods and walks out.

I place his mother's letters into the kitchen sink and put a match to them. As they burn to ashes, I tell myself that now nobody—not Sebastian's nemesis, not even me in a moment of anger—will be able to punch him where it hurts most.

# TWENTY-SIX

We're in the home stretch.

If Sebastian's nemesis doesn't make his move *really* soon, my fake husband of one month and I will go on a break, separate and divorce, pretexting irreconcilable differences.

Sebastian is getting a little nervous about the success of his plan.

I would be, too, in his place.

All his efforts of the past six months, the elaborate deception of family and friends, the marriage to a woman he'd never consider wife material, the luxury wedding, extravagant parties, and lavish receptions—it's all been for naught. To say nothing of the money he's still to fork over when my payday arrives.

If nothing out of the ordinary happens this week, I'll pocket my fee and leave next week. Sebastian will go back to his normal life, none the wiser. And his enemy will thank his lucky stars for having stayed under the radar.

No wonder my still-husband is cramming as many opportunities for his enemy as he can into this last week. The first one is underway right now, and it's a happy event, regardless of our hidden agenda.

Jeanne's hubby, Mat, was elected Member of the European Parliament, as the *Top-of-the-List* for the Greens.

Sebastian had backed his party's campaign, so he's doubly pleased.

To celebrate Mat's achievement, we're hosting a big reception at Raphael and Sebastian's gentlemen's club. Mat wanted to do it at *La Bohème*, but the bistro was too small for the occasion. Everyone who's anyone in Paris and from Mat's home base in Normandy is here, schmoozing, drinking, and stuffing themselves with caviar canapés.

Sebastian steers the event with his usual efficiency, making sure Mat meets all the movers and shakers and opinion leaders.

I play the perfect hostess—at least, my idea of the perfect hostess. Dressed in a shimmery gown that feels and looks as if it was poured on me, I welcome and make small talk with as many guests as I can manage without appearing rushed.

As I do my rounds, I notice Sebastian chatting with a creature who should totally represent France at the next Miss Universe. They smile at each other, the distance between them considerably smaller than what's expected of two people holding a polite conversation. She plays with her earlobe as she speaks. Sebastian beckons to a server and picks up two champagne flutes.

A needle of jealousy pricks me somewhere in the upper left quadrant of my chest, but I will myself to ignore it and carry on.

One of the uniformed waitresses carrying a tray with food and drinks keeps glancing at Raphael. The depth of her gaze is intriguing. Every time she steals a glance at him, something flashes in her pretty eyes—something bigger than just *OMG-what-a-studmuffin*. Her furtive looks have an undeniable gravitas that goes beyond flirtation. It suggests a history. And a *complicated* one, at that.

When I spot Manon, I rush to her side for a chat that I'll actually enjoy.

"Where's Amar, by the way?" I ask after we've covered her recent raise and the encouraging sales of my new prints at *La Bohème*. "I haven't seen him yet."

She looks down, visibly distressed.

"What's wrong? Is he OK?"

"I don't know."

I give her a quizzical look.

"He's disappeared."

"What do you mean?"

"He's gone," she says. "It's been three days now. He hasn't showed up for work, and he won't return my calls."

"Are you going to report his disappearance to the police?"

She shakes her head. "I managed to get hold of his mom. She says Amar left the country."

"Why?"

"I couldn't get anything else out of her." There's a tremor in her voice. "I'm at my wit's end."

I give her a hug. "He'll come back. He loves you."

"I'm not... I'm not so sure anymore."

Someone taps my shoulder. "Here she is, the beautiful hostess of this great celebration!"

I turn around—it's Sebastian's pal, Laurent.

"Thank you for the 'beautiful,' " I say as we cheek kiss. "I hope you're enjoying yourself."

"Absolutely." He tilts his head toward Manon. "Will you introduce me to your equally beautiful friend?"

I do and leave them to it. God knows, Manon could do with a distraction right now.

Besides, I really need to pee.

Just as I'm opening the door to the ladies' room, Raphael and the glancing waitress come out of the gents' toilet. He's tucking his shirt into his pants. She's smoothing her uniform. Both are rumpled and flushed, leaving no doubt about what they were doing in the men's bathroom.

Or about the nature of their "history."

When I return to the front room, there are daggers flying around. Not material ones, of course, but the looks Genevieve is giving the waitress. They're so sharp it's a miracle her victim isn't screaming in pain and collapsing to the floor.

I smirk.

Raphael may believe that Genevieve is only a friend, but the truth is she may as well be wearing a T-shirt that reads, *Hands off the middle Darcy brother—HE'S MINE.*

Men can be so selectively blind!

Sebastian comes over to me. "Did you see the woman I've been talking to for the past thirty minutes?"

"I did."

"We've already *bumped* into each other at the Chanel luncheon I attended for work last week." His eyes are bright with excitement.

"Do you think…" I search his face. "Do you think she's it?"

"I just texted the PI to stand by outside."

"What happens next?"

He looks at his watch. "In an hour or so, people will start leaving. You'll say you're tired and go home."

"And you?"

"If all goes well, I'll leave with my temptress."

I'm itching to ask if he'll do more than just "leave" with her. For his scheme to work, I guess he'll need to. The question is how far he'll go. Will he just drive her home, kiss her, and let his private eye shadow her until she contacts her employer, or will he actually go all the way and sleep with her?

He's never been very specific on that part of the plan.

I nod and force myself to smile. "Fingers crossed."

"Don't wait up for me tonight," he says.

That needle I'd felt earlier morphs into a dirty bomb and blows up inside my chest just as Sebastian turns and walks away.

# Part V
# Hovel

# TWENTY-SEVEN

How hard can it be to open a pair of healthy, well-functioning eyes? Right now, extremely hard. Almost impossible. It's not just the eyes. My head is pounding. Nausea reigns supreme in my stomach, threatening to advance through my throat and erupt at any moment.

How much exactly did I drink last night? Barely a glass. I was too busy playing hostess. So why am I having the hangover of my life? I try to rub my eyes, but my hands won't come up. A few more failed attempts later and it hits me. My wrists are bound behind my back. My ankles are tied, too.

*What the hell?*

With a superhuman effort, I peel my eyes open and take in my surroundings. I'm lying on top of a mattress in a dark, moldy-smelling room. Probably a cellar. I writhe and buck, testing the strength of the tape at my wrists and ankles. It's impossible to untie or even loosen a little. After some more wriggling, I manage to sit up, lean back against the wall, and look around.

It *is* a cellar. It's small, so I doubt I'm in the mansion, where I've thoroughly explored the huge basement. There's a minuscule opening just below the ceiling. That's where the air and light come through. A suitcase sits in one corner of the room. My suitcase. The wall opposite me has a door with no handle. I don't like that door any more than I like the window covered with a solid metal screen.

Clearly, at some point between the moment Greg dropped me off in front of Darcy House and now, I passed out and was brought down here.

Did someone hit me over the head? Drug me? Hypnotize me?

The thing is I have no memory of it.

I call for help, scream, call for help again, and then scream some more.

Nothing happens.

I call for help a few more times.

The door opens. A sturdy man steps in and locks the door behind him. He pauses for a moment by the door and then walks slowly toward me.

Recognition slaps me on the face like a bucket of icy water.

"I hope *madame* slept well," Octave says, mockery palpable in his voice. "I hope you weren't too cold and your restraints not too tight."

He halts in front of me.

I give him a long, hard stare. "It's been you—all this time, pretending to be a friend and sharpening your knife behind Sebastian's back."

"I was never his *friend*," Octave hisses. "I'm his *majordome*, remember?"

"What do you want?" I ask.

"I'm not sure yet." He gives me the smile of a deranged man. "I'm considering different scenarios."

"What about Miss France at the bash last night? Wasn't she supposed to seduce Sebastian? Wasn't that your plan?"

He throws his head back and roars with an uncontrollable laugher, tears and all. "Is that what you both thought? I was hoping you would."

Octave pulls a hanky from his pocket and wipes his eyes. "She was just a diversion."

I blink, processing that piece of information.

"You see," he says. "I had to adapt my initial plan after you moved in."

"Why?"

"Because I heard Sebastian and you talking one night, between humping sessions, about outing his nemesis."

"You—what? How?"

"I bugged your bedroom."

*Dear Lord.*

That explains the device and headphones in his closet.

*I'm toast.*

Unless… The bugging might be good news. It means he's discovered the truth about us.

"In that case," I say, "you know our marriage is a sham."

"What?" He looks genuinely surprised.

"If you've bugged our bedroom, you must've figured out from our conversations that we're not for real. Sebastian hired me to help him unmask you."

He sneers. "Nice try."

"It's the truth."

"You really expect me to believe your bullshit?"

I close my eyes and try to concentrate. Could it be that neither Sebastian nor I ever said anything in that bedroom that would give away the real nature of our relationship? We've had a lot of sex, many laughs, and a few serious conversations, but… is it possible that we never mentioned our contract?

But of course, we did—as recently as two weeks ago. Only we weren't in Darcy House. We were in my apartment.

Octave squats and checks the tape at my wrists and ankles.

"I may be just a manservant, but I'm not stupid," he says. "I've seen the way you look at him—like he's the only man on the whole fucking planet. I've seen the way he looks at you—like he wants to nosh you for breakfast, lunch, and dinner every fucking day."

I take a ragged breath and look away.

"And don't get me started on the way he touches you." Octave stands up, smirking. "These things can't be faked."

I lick my dry lips, realizing how parched I am.

Octave turns around and heads to the door.

"Wait," I call after him.

He halts and looks over his shoulder at me.

I point my chin to the suitcase. "What's that for?"

"To buy me a few days. He'll think you got jealous and left him."

In a few days, I'll be dead from dehydration. That is if he doesn't kill me before.

"Will you please bring me some water next time you come down?" I ask.

"No," he says. "I'm not your servant anymore, sweetheart."

# TWENTY-EIGHT

I get home in the wee hours of the morning.

Valeria—that's my temptress's name… fake, no doubt—wanted to go to her favorite nightclub. She *loooooves* dancing. After that she asked me to take her for a ride around the Boulogne Forest, driving my Lamborghini as fast as it would go. She *adooooores* speed.

When I took her back to her hotel, she invited me upstairs for a "cup of coffee." That's when I went off script and declined her invitation.

"Wife?" She gave me a sympathetic look.

I nodded.

Valeria pointed at her watch. "It's three in the morning. She won't believe you anyway."

"I'll try my luck." I planted a quick smooch on her lips and promised I'd make arrangements so we could meet again soon without raising anyone's suspicions.

She gave me her number and told me to use it anytime.

I drove off, praying she wouldn't wait too long before contacting her employer. Despite her striking beauty, I really don't care for the prospect of "meeting her again soon."

Right now, what I long for is sleep. Next to Diane. I picture myself performing what's become my favorite bedtime ritual. It consists of spooning Diane to my chest, wrapping an arm around her, and breathing in the skin at her nape.

It occurs to me as I climb the stairs to the second floor that I haven't had a single sleepless night since she's been sharing my bed.

I also realize that what I told her the other day about not wanting a relationship with her was, as she'd say, a big pile of shit.

Treading as lightly as possible so I don't wake her up, I enter the bedroom—and know at once that she's gone. I turn on the light and look around. The bed hasn't been turned down. Her nightstand is free of her baubles. I rush to the walk-in closet. One of her suitcases and some of her clothes are missing.

She's left me.

Why? Up until now, she'd stuck to our deal remarkably well. Why quit now before we have proof that my plan has worked, before our contract has expired, and before we've had a chance to discuss this new development?

Was it jealousy?

I've suspected for some time now that Diane has feelings for me, but I didn't think they were strong. And I certainly didn't think she'd let them cloud her judgement.

I sit down on the bed and drop my head into my hands, disappointment washing through me in cold, sticky waves. The funny thing is I'm more upset about Diane's walking out on me than jeopardizing my plan. Her departure makes the prospect of a future without her real for the first time.

That future holds no witty commentary on everything under the sun, no adorable goofiness, and no refreshing disregard for my money and status.

Nor does it hold lovemaking that's been growing sweeter every night, instead of palling.

I'd believed a future without Diane Petit was what I wanted.

But all I can see in it now is bleakness.

Depressing, morbid, unbearable bleakness.

*What have I done?*

In the quiet of the house, the sound of a door unlocking and gently closing comes from the foyer. I jump up and run down the stairs, tripping on the carpet, getting up, and running again. Is it Diane? Has she changed her mind? Did she reconsider the wisdom of her actions?

Let it be her. Please, let it be her.

But it's only Octave—the last person in this household I expected to come home at this hour.

He smiles apologetically. "I hope I didn't wake monsieur up."

"No, I was awake." I hesitate. "Have you seen Diane?"

He shakes his head. "Didn't she come home with you?"

"No," I say drily. "She didn't."

I wish Octave good night and return to my bedroom, which feels awfully empty without my lover.

When I crawl into bed fifteen minutes later, I lie on her side and bury my nose in her pillow.

*I'm a fool.*

Blinded by Diane's charm, I was beginning to convince myself she could be the right woman for me—a partner for life, my anchor, my rock. Drunk on her body, I was beginning to see her as the woman who'd stay by my side through good times and bad, sickness and health, society obligations and job demands, babies to be raised and mistakes to be forgiven.

*I'm such a pathetic fool.*

# TWENTY-NINE

It's my second day in Octave's cellar.

I shift my position to sit a little more comfortably and close my eyes. My mouth and lips are on fire. I'm dizzy and so tired I can barely think.

Tyrion's words from *Game of Thrones* come to my mind: "Death is so terribly final, while life is full of possibilities."

With the prospect of death a lot closer to home than when I watched the series with Chloe, I've been thinking a lot about possibilities. My favorite one is code named *Clean Slate*. It goes like this: Sebastian Darcy isn't the filthy-rich fragrance mogul who ruined Dad. It was his main competitor, David Bauer, who did it.

*Dreaming here, remember?*

Actually, no one has ruined Dad. His business is doing well, he didn't suffer a stroke, and he and Mom are still together. Sebastian exposes Octave, thanks to his formidable powers of deduction. This means he doesn't need to hire me—or anyone—to be his fake wife.

We meet in the most conventional way at Jeanne and Mat's, and we fall in love. Just like that—*Bam!*—at first sight. It doesn't matter that he reads *Le Figaro* and is worth more than the GDP of a small country.

Nobody's perfect.

We date, kiss, make love, make babies, and live happily ever after.

I open my eyes and stare at the door.

*He'll find me.*

Just as he found me after the cake incident, which now seems like a lifetime ago. If there's something I've learned about him, it's that Sebastian Darcy won't just shrug at my sudden departure and move on. He'll want to know why I left. He'll call. He'll poke around, talk to Mom, Chloe, and Elorie.

And he'll end up figuring it out.

*I must believe it.*

The alternative is to give up and stop struggling to stay alive even before Octave turns up to finish me off.

The door opens and Octave comes in.

"Have you made up your mind about me?" I ask, my voice coarse.

"I had last night," he says. "I was going to come here and strangle you. But then I lost my nerve."

I look into his eyes. "Bummer."

"You're funny, you know?" He lets out a sigh. "It *is* a bummer."

"Tell me something, Octave—just so I don't die stupid—why?"

"Why what?"

"Why are you doing this? Why are you going to such pains to punish the person who thinks the world of you?"

"Does he now?" Octave smirks. "He *is* less full of himself than his legendary Grandpa Bernard, and his adored papa. I'll grant you that."

An image flashes in my head when he mentions Sebastian's grandfather—that of Octave's birth certificate.

"Your middle name is Bernard," I say.

The side of his face twitches. "So what?"

"It isn't a coincidence, is it? Your hatred of the d'Arcy men… it has something to do with your middle name, I'm sure."

"Not only are you funny," he says. "You're also perceptive."

I wait for him to continue.

Because he will. The man is clearly burning to tell his story to *someone*. He's been burning for years, decades maybe. And now he has an ideal audience: captive, genuinely interested, and expendable.

He'd have to be made of steel to resist that.

"Bernard d'Arcy had a fling with my mother when they were both young," he says.

*I knew it!*

"It was more than a fling, actually. They were together for over a year until he ditched her and married the fancy-schmancy Colette."

"What did your mother do?"

"She up and married a good-for-nothing from her hometown. And then she had me."

"Are you Bernard's son?" I ask.

He sighs. "I don't know. My mother always denied it, but she never got over Bernard and she did give me that middle name. Besides, she wrote to him when I turned eighteen, asking if he could offer me a job at Parfums d'Arcy."

"Did he?"

"He offered me a job at Darcy House instead." Octave runs his hand through his thinning hair, his expression melancholy. "I was over the moon. I thought it was a sign that the Count was willing to take me under his wing, maybe even acknowledge me one day... I was so naive."

"I take it he didn't acknowledge you?"

Octave shakes his head. "Worse. He never even bothered to get to know me, let alone groom me for bigger things. He groomed Thibaud, all right, and then Sebastian. But never me."

"Did you ever talk to him about your mother?"

"I didn't dare. He was so distant, so much above me… We weren't equals. He was Count d'Arcy du Grand-Thouars de Saint-Maurice. I was the help."

"Why didn't you walk away?" I ask. "Once you knew Bernard would never treat you like a son, why didn't you just leave?"

My mouth and throat hurt from talking, and I'm extremely tired but still lucid enough to remember that as long as Octave is telling his story, he isn't strangling me.

"At first, I had hope," he says. "I thought if I proved myself to him, if I showed him how good and loyal I could be, he'd let me in. I tried so hard, for so long… And then, when I accepted that I'd never earn his love, it was too late. I'd become too appreciative of the grandeur of Darcy House and the comforts of my life to quit everything and start over."

"So instead you chose to stay and poison their lives," I say.

"Exactly." Octave puts his chin up. "My mother died around the same time, and I made a promise on her grave. I vowed I'd make the lives of Bernard, Thibaud, and Sebastian miserable without risking my freedom or my job."

"My hat's off to you," I say. "You succeeded."

He gives me a smug smile. "Yes, I did."

For a moment, we're both silent. Then Octave's eyes dart to my neck. *Oh no.* I must get him to start talking again—and presto!

"Have you done a DNA test to find out who your father is?" I ask.

He shakes his head. "I can't."

"Why not?"

He hesitates and then shrugs as if to say, *What the hell, I might as well be honest with the soon-to-be-dead woman.* "I'm too scared. What if the test says I'm not related to the d'Arcys? Do you realize the implications?" He points at me. "Your... end, Thibaud's disgrace, Sebastian's grief—it would all be for nothing. Meaningless. I wouldn't be able to handle it."

"And you think you'll be able to handle *murdering* me?" I ask.

He opens his mouth to say something when the door bursts open and a bunch of police officers in bulletproof vests storm in. Two of them slam Octave to the floor and cuff him. The others rush to me and cut my restraints.

It all seems surreal. A few moments later, I'm wrapped in a blanket and carried up the stairs into the daylight.

Sebastian runs to me and takes me in his arms. He's crying.

"You're alive," he says, raining kisses on my cheeks, eyes, nose, and forehead. "You're alive!"

I start crying, too.

"Shush, *mon amour*," he says in a hot whisper, kissing away my tears. "You're safe now. It's over. I'm here. You're safe."

# THIRTY

"I signed up for meditation and yoga." Mom turns to Chloe. "And I might call your therapist as well."

Chloe smiles. "It won't hurt."

Mom takes my hand. "First Chloe in October, now you… Please—both of you—don't scare me like that ever again."

I nudge her lemonade glass across the garden table. "You should taste it. Michel makes it from a medieval recipe he guards with his life."

She takes a sip and swishes it around in her mouth before swallowing. "Mine is better."

An hour later, they're gone and I recline on the deck chair for a nap. I've been sleeping a lot over the past two days, which is weird because I hadn't been exactly *active* during the preceding forty-eight hours.

When I wake up, I find Sebastian sitting on the grass at my feet.

"It's Wednesday," I say. "Shouldn't you be at the office, bossing people around?"

He kisses my ankles. "I'd rather be here."

"I need to stretch my legs," I say.

He jumps to his feet and helps me up.

As we stroll through the garden, I brush my hand over tree branches and shrubbery, caressing the leaves. Everything smells so good, looks so beautiful, feels so pleasant to touch… God, I'm happy I made it.

"Mom told me you went on TV, offering a ransom," I say.

He nods.

"She says you didn't specify an amount—you just said, 'Name your price, I'll pay it.' "

He nods again.

I give him a sidelong look. "Don't you think that was a little presumptuous?"

He shakes his head.

I'm itching to ask whether he'd have paid up if Octave had demanded a billion euros.

"I would've given everything I have," he says. "Don't you ever doubt that."

I stop and hug him, burying my face against his chest. He puts his arms around me and kisses the top of my head. There are so many things I want to say to him, but they're all too sentimental for my cynical mouth. So I hug him tighter instead, hoping he'll understand.

Praying that he knows.

"When did you first suspect foul play?" I ask after a long moment.

"Sunday morning. I called you a dozen times. I called Elorie, Chloe, and your Mom. When your Mom said she hadn't seen or heard from you, I knew you hadn't just upped and left."

"Thank God you didn't call Dad, and thank God he doesn't own a TV," I say.

"Chloe was very helpful. She called him for a chat and ascertained that you weren't with him."

We walk in silence for a few minutes. I listen to the birds in the trees and insects humming around us. But I have too many questions to fully enjoy the peaceful magic of this place.

"When did you start suspecting Octave?"

"Sometime Sunday night. I tossed and turned, and then I remembered him coming in at four a.m. the night you disappeared."

"Powers of deduction," I say under my breath.

"Pardon me?"

"Nothing." I wave my hand dismissively. "Just a side effect of having only me to entertain myself for two days straight."

He puts his hand around my shoulders.

"What did you do once you had your suspicions?" I ask.

"I texted my PI to forget Valerie and start tailing Octave ASAP. Then I dressed and drove to the nearest *commissariat*."

"Thank goodness you didn't call the police or your PI from home. Octave had the bedroom bugged."

Sebastian stops in his tracks, his jaw clenched in anger.

"Finish your story," I ask.

"Things went pretty fast from there," he says. "On Monday morning, the police figured out Octave had inherited a hovel in Yvelines, an hour's drive from Paris. That's when the PI texted me that he was driving behind my *majordome* in that same direction."

Sebastian trails off, his gaze suddenly unfocused.

"You OK?" I ask.

"Yes, of course. It just hit me how, at one point or another, I've suspected everyone—my competitors, my aunt and uncle, Greg, Lynette... even Laurent! But I never doubted Octave." His nostrils flare. "How could I be so blind? It almost cost you your life."

"But it didn't." I give him a bright smile. "You got there on time. You found me."

"I love you, Diane," he says. "With all my heart."

I sort of figured that out but, dear Lord, it's good to hear him say those words!

"I love you, too, Sebastian."

He takes my left hand and strokes my ring finger. "You're still wearing your engagement ring and your wedding band."

"Oh." I pull my hand away and begin to remove the jewelry. "Silly me! We don't need them anymore now that—"

"Don't!" He takes hold of my hand again and pushes the rings back to the base of my finger. "Will you do me the honor of remaining my wife?"

My jaw drops.

He smiles. "Your spontaneity is priceless. Please don't ever change."

I keep silent, still digesting his words.

"Say yes," he pleads.

"I don't understand," I say instead. "What do you mean by 'remaining your wife'? Our marriage is fake."

He shakes his head. "Not if I send the missing document to the consulate in Miami. We still have two weeks until the deadline."

"I can't." I say. "It would be against what I profess, against my principles."

"Which are…?"

I focus on my feet. "I hate rich people. They're all exploiters and crooks. I don't believe it's possible to amass a fortune by being a good person."

"Diane." He takes my chin between his index finger and thumb, nudging me gently to look at him. "I don't care what you think of 'rich people' as a class. However, I do care what you think of me. Do you believe I'm an exploiter and a crook?"

"No," I say without a second's hesitation. "I don't. Ludicrous as it is, I think you're a good person."

The corners of his mouth curl up. "You sure?"

"Yes. And I have proof."

"You do?"

I nod. "It was you who 'persuaded' Belle Auxbois to go on prime-time TV and credit Dad for her perfume. Now he has so many offers he's raised his fee and established a waiting list." I grip Sebastian's hand and give it a squeeze. "Thank you."

"How did you—"

"It doesn't matter." I bring his hand to my lips and kiss it. "And there's something else. When I told him who was behind Belle's sudden generosity, he admitted you'd offered to buy his company before you crushed it."

"I thought you knew about it," he says.

I shake my head.

He strokes my hands and touches my engagement ring. "Do you like it? Or shall I get you a new one, something *you* would choose? We could go to Place Vendôme tomorrow—"

"No!" I cut him off. "I mean, I wouldn't mind something less ritzy, but that's not what I... It's just... How..."

He tilts his head to the side, waiting for me to form my question.

"What would be the terms?" I finally manage.

"Let's see." He opens the thumb of his left hand. "You'll have to kiss me. A lot." He extends his index finger. "You'll have to sleep in my bed, and you'll be expected to have sex with me—both in and out of that bed."

I smile and roll my eyes skyward.

He uncurls his middle finger. "You'll call me 'my beloved spouse' in public and 'my stallion' in private."

I stick my finger in my mouth and pretend to gag.

"It was a joke," he says.

"You sure?"

He nods vigorously.

I pretend to wipe my brow. "Phew."

"But this one isn't." He unfolds his ring finger. "I'll expect you to be my teammate. I'll need you to stand by my side through everything and support me in running the company and the house, regardless of your leftist ideology."

I draw in a deep breath.

"And this one isn't a joke, either." Sebastian opens his little finger, eyes burning into mine. "I'll be the happiest of men if you give me a child. A few, if possible."

I swallow and hold his gaze.

He smiles again. "That's it. Those are the terms. Do you think you can do those things for me?"

"I think I can," I say. "And then some."

His smile grows into a huge grin.

"But," I say, taking his hand. "What I meant by 'terms' was actually of a more... *financial* nature. You and I are too unequal in that regard."

He says nothing.

"Do you have a prenup contract drafted?" I ask.

He shakes his head. "We don't need one."

"You've lost your mind."

"Quite the contrary." He lifts my hand to his lips and plants a hot kiss to my palm. "I've found it."

I look down, thinking.

"Say yes, Diane." He gives my hand a squeeze.

I lift my eyes. "On one condition."

"Anything."

"You'll pose for me naked again. Every time I ask you to."

He arches an eyebrow.

I put my hand to my heart. "For strictly personal use, I promise."

"OK," he says. "But I'll be your *only* male model."

"Deal."

He nods. "Deal."

"Then it's a yes." I throw my arms around his neck and add in a husky voice, "My stallion."

# Author's Note

If you enjoyed this book, please consider posting a short (or long) review on Amazon or GoodReads to help others discover it.

Thank you!
Alix

# Bonus Chapters

### Raphael's Fling
*(The Darcy Brothers)*

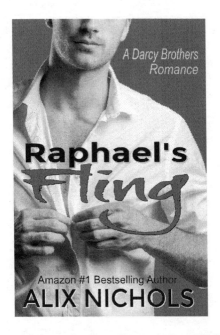

**One bookish assistant. One cocky CEO. One Christmas party that changes everything. ~ ~ ~**

*I'm Mia, and I dream about publishing a guide to medieval Paris. Except... I'm better qualified for writing a manual on how to go from a budding scholar to a pregnant runaway in three easy steps.*

# Chapter One

*How did I come to this?*

I sigh, smooth my clothes one last time, and head for the cream, leather-padded door.

"Mia, wait!" Raphael calls after me.

I halt and turn around.

He opens his chiseled mouth as if to say something, then shuts it, and gives me a tight smile. The smile of a person having second thoughts on the advisability of what he was going to say.

Well, I'm not waiting around for the result of his inner deliberation. There are two bulky reports on my desk and a few dozen emails I need to go through before I can leave tonight.

Ergo, time is of the essence.

I resume my hike across Raphael's vast office until I reach the door. It unlocks smoothly and without a sound, bless its high-tech heart. After a sneak peek in the hall to check if the coast is clear, I slip away without saying good-bye to Raphael or Anne-Marie, his faithful PA.

*Just like a lawbreaker.*

Well, maybe not a lawbreaker, but definitely a reoffending violator of the *Workplace Code of Honor.* In particular, of Rule #1, which says: "Workers shall not have sexual intercourse with their hierarchical superiors, inferiors, or posteriors."

While there's some controversy over the exact meaning of "inferiors" and "posteriors," everyone knows that a "superior" is more than just your immediate boss. The concept also covers your boss's boss, your boss's boss's boss's boss, and the Boss of Them All—the CEO.

It's a very sensible provision, by the way, and one I totally approve of and adhere to.

As I rush down the hallway, my heels clicking on the marble floor, I realize I should've put my observation in the past tense. As in, "I *used* to adhere to."

Having repeatedly broken the Code's first rule since March makes me a rogue and a hypocrite of the worst kind.

*How did I fall so low?*

Here's a clue: it's Rudolph the Reindeer's fault.

God knows I hadn't planned on this when I landed the world's most unexceptional job as assistant to the daily bulletin editor at DCA Paris. DCA stands for "D'Arcy Consulting and Audit." Yup, the same "d'Arcy" that's sandwiched between "Raphael" and the rest of his fancy name on my lover's official letterhead.

Having sexual intercourse with Raphael d'Arcy du Grand-Thouars de Saint-Maurice, a gentleman and a libertine, was the last thing on my mind when I started at DCA. In fact, it was nowhere *near* my mind.

Despite my murky past, that's not who I am. Nor does my life need more complications right now.

*Trust me.*

Pauline Cordier's familiar silhouette takes shape at the end of the hallway just as I reach the elevator and push the button. My heart skips a beat. If my direct supervisor sees me on this floor, she'll assume one of the following two things: (a) my presence here is work-related, meaning I'm going over her head; or (b) my presence here has nothing to do with work, meaning I'm sleeping with one of the senior managers.

Needless to say, both alternatives are equally conducive to me getting sidelined, ostracized, and ultimately fired.

I take a deep breath and give the approaching figure a furtive glance.

It isn't Pauline.

The woman doesn't even look like her, now that she's closer.

*Phew.*

You may not believe me, but I wasn't sure what Raphael d'Arcy looked like when DCA hired me. Having scanned his official bio in preparation for my job interview, I had formed a vague image that boiled down to "young, well-born, and well-dressed." The specifics of the founding CEO's background and appearance hadn't lingered in my mind. I doubt they'd even entered it.

Because they were not important.

All I wanted from Monsieur d'Arcy was a job at his firm that gave me a monthly paycheck to complement the pittance my school calls a scholarship. That way, I could finish my doctoral program without having to sleep under bridges or borrow money.

Parisian bridges can be drafty, you see. And damp. As for the stench, courtesy of well-groomed dogs and ill-groomed humans, don't even get me started! On top of all that, bridges offer no suitable storage space for research notes, photocopies, and books.

In short, they suck as accommodations.

As for the borrowing, my parents taught Eva and me that debt must be avoided at all costs. Their "debt is bad" precept proved stronger than the knowledge that everyone lives on credit in Western societies today.

Except my parents, that is.

Then again, they live in rural Alsace. Life's a lot cheaper there than in *la capitale*, so they were able to make it into their fifties without a single loan to cloud their horizon.

I step off the elevator on the second floor, relieved that no one saw me in Top Management's Heavenly Quarters, and my phone rings. Considering that I've been sneaking out like this for two months already, the probability that someone *will* see me and that it'll reach Pauline's ears is growing by the day.

It freaks me out more than I care to admit.

As I answer the phone, Raphael's deep, sexy timbre breaks me from my worries.

"You left your panties here," he says, sounding

amused and smug at the same time. In short, his usual self.

"No, I didn't—"

*Oh crap.* I did.

"I've got five minutes before the managerial," he says, "so if you want to come back and collect—"

"No!" I look around and lower my voice. "It's OK. I'm sure I can make it through the afternoon without them."

"Oh, I don't doubt that. The question is whether *I* can make it through the afternoon *with* the knowledge you're *without* them." He pauses, as if pondering the question, and then adds, "And *with* them in my pocket."

My stomach flips.

Something achingly—yet delightfully—heavy gathers low in my abdomen, reminding me of what Raphael and I had been up to a mere half hour ago. Suddenly, every step I take makes me aware of my pantyless condition. The friction of my skirt's silky lining against my bare skin makes it prickle. My breathing becomes strained, and my heart thumps in my chest.

As I struggle to calm myself before entering the office I share with two other assistants, I picture myself in Strasbourg in our family physician's immaculate office.

"What's my diagnosis, doctor?" I'd ask after he's examined me.

"Not to worry, *mon enfant!* You'll live." He'd

push his regular glasses to his forehead and put on his reading glasses. "You have a textbook case of *lustium irresistiblum*."

"Please, can you make it go away?"

He'd smile and shake his head, updating my file on his computer. "It's like a viral cold. It'll clear up on its own, eventually."

And that, my friends, is the second clue to the mystery of how I got here.

It appears I've caught a virulent strain of *lustium irresistiblum* for lady-killer Raphael d'Arcy. And with my luck, we'll likely get caught before it clears.

"Got to go," I whisper into the phone and hang up.

I take a few long breaths to chase my arousal away before I enter the office.

Easier said than done.

The things Raphael says, the things he does to me... They don't just *excite*—they break into my brain and muddle it up on a deep, molecular level. Throwing ethical norms against that kind of invasion has been as effective as attempting to shoot down the Death Star with foam darts.

But I'll keep on trying.

Till the bitter end.

# TWO

I spent the first month at DCA Paris without a single sighting of *Le Big Boss*, as the assistants in my department call him. This is not surprising, considering the six floors and about as many layers of hierarchy that separate us. If we had ever bumped into each other in a hallway, he wouldn't have known me from a bar of soap and I wouldn't have recognized him.

Then the traditional Christmas party arrived. The organizing committee decreed it would be a costume event, and anyone who dared to turn up without a proper disguise would be sent home.

By a stroke of luck or misfortune, I happened to own an old costume just perfect for a Christmas party—Rudolph the Red-Nosed Reindeer. It was a fluffy onesie that came with a set of antlers adorning its roomy hood that covered the top half of my face and an elastic-band red nose. The costume had been in my parents' attic since I'd graduated high school. It begged to be worn again.

*I shouldn't have listened to its pleas!*

Had I known where that brown faux-fur onesie would land me, I would've never worn it to the office Christmas party. Heck, I would've never gone to that party to start with! But in the absence of a crystal ball to foresee the future, Rudolph had seemed like a great idea.

When I entered the meeting room, which had been transformed into a dance floor complete with a disco ball, it looked anything but Christmassy. Scantily clad Santa babes, provocative elves, and seductive angels—to say nothing of Playboy Bunnies—were gulping down champagne and undulating their lithe bodies to the beat of "I Know You Want Me." Many of them were also singing along and winking at their dance partners, *I know you want me, You know I want cha.*

Their male coworkers weren't far behind. They sported costumes representing an assortment of shoulder-padded Marvel superheroes with an occasional bare-chested Santa thrown in. Nearly every one of them drank, danced, and flirted with the ferocity of someone determined to get lucky.

In other words, much fun was being had.

"The name of the game is *Locate Le Big Boss*," my office mate Delphine said, handing me a glass of bubbly.

A champagne cork shot through the air, a little too close for comfort to my face. I ducked, spilling the contents of my flute and making Delphine chuckle.

Straightening up, I looked around. "Maybe he isn't even here."

"Word on the street says he is." Delphine winked, refilling my flute. "Barb and I have been trying to figure out which Iron Man he is, based on stature and voice."

"Personally, I think he's neither," a tutu-clad black swan said, planting herself next to us.

Upon closer examination, the swan was Tanya, a junior auditor famous for her illustrious conquests.

"Personally, I think he's Père Noël over there." Tanya pointed at the tall, fully dressed Father Christmas stroking his white beard and chatting with two Playboy Bunnies in the corner of the room.

"You may be right," Delphine said, contemplating the group. "I've heard Raphael's latest fling was one of those ménage à trois deals that every man dreams about."

I smirked. "So you think he's trying for an encore?"

"The hell he is." Tanya put her chin up and pulled down her areola-revealing top. "His next fling will be *me*."

With that, she strode toward Père Noël, her head high and her step bouncy. I couldn't help picturing her firing at will from her jutting boobs, decimating the bunnies, and snagging *Le Big Boss*.

At least for the night.

"Have fun, *ma cocotte,*" Delphine said to me, moving away to greet a newcomer.

I marched away from the champagne cork crossfire and imminent Bunny Massacre. Since I hadn't the slightest intention of locating Raphael d'Arcy, I stayed away from superheroes and Santas the entire evening, gravitating toward the older and more conservatively dressed colleagues. At some point, I danced with a fellow onesie-clad snowman who had an oversized carrot for a nose. But mostly, I sipped champagne and talked politics with the over-fifty crowd.

The problem was said crowd thinned quickly after midnight. By one in the morning, it became hard to find someone more interested in having a conversation than in making out. Not that anyone—male or female—would want to make out with Rudolph the Red-Nosed Reindeer.

My second problem was that I was growing increasingly warm and uncomfortable in my faux-fur costume. I would've left—*I should've left!*—then and there, but Delphine and I had agreed to share a cab ride home, seeing as we live in the same arrondissement.

Unfortunately, by the time I was ready to leave, Delphine was engrossed in an advanced flirtation with The Hulk, who looked a lot like her longtime crush, Alberto.

There was no way she was leaving now.

I sighed, refilled my flute, and stepped out onto the dark balcony. Removing my red nose, I turned my face up to let the fresh December air cool it. Five minutes later, I was having a blast all by myself on the balcony, which was more of a terrace, as far as I could make out in the dark. My body temperature had dropped, and my champagne-soaked brain had cleared enough to realize that the random balcony I'd escaped to offered the best view of Paris I'd ever seen.

My night was beginning to look up.

Looking out over the parapet, I downed my champagne and admired the brightly lit city when someone stumbled out and came to stand next to me.

It was the snowman I'd danced with earlier.

He gave me a nod and touched his beer bottle to

my flute. "To your good health."

"And to yours," I said, trying to figure out how drunk he was.

And if I was peeved or pleased at his arrival.

*Peeved*, I decided. *Definitely*.

Unlike us staid reindeer, snowmen were fickle creatures.

They could melt down on you any time.

*End of Excerpt*

# *Amanda's Guide to Love*

## *(La Bohème Series)*

*Parisian career woman Amanda Roussel lives in denial of her desperate loneliness.*

*Gypsy gambler Kes Moreno knows he's in trouble when he falls for Amanda after a one-night stand.*

*Can he convince the snarky belle they're right for each other?*

~~~

# Chapter One
## Rock Bottom

*A Woman's Guide to Perfection*
*Guideline # 1*
**The Perfect Woman doesn't do one-night stands.**

*Rationale*: One-night stands (ONS) are always disappointing, often hazardous, and invariably awkward.

*A word of caution*: If you are a frequent ONSer, shut this book right now and give it to someone who may benefit from it. You will never be a Perfect Woman. *Ever*.

*Permissible exception*: A prolonged dry spell between boyfriends or a highly stressful life event.

*Damage control*: (a) make sure the sex is safe, (b) make sure your person is safe, (c) leave or kick him or her out before breakfast, (d) wash your body squeaky clean, (e) scrub the memory of the episode from your brain.

*Pitfalls to avoid:* (a) giving him or her your phone number, (b) telling your best friend about it, (c) thinking that a one-night stand could ever lead to a relationship.

~ ~ ~

Amanda stared at the typed letter. Neatly strung words zoomed in and out of focus as their meaning sank in. *Mademoiselle Roussel . . . I regret to inform you . . . with immediate effect.*

She swallowed hard and slipped the letter into her purse.

Most of her colleagues would cheer at the news. They'd rush into each other's offices and say, "Did you hear? Viper Tongue got the sack! Serves her right." Some of them might send around an e-mail invite for a celebratory drink. Others would just shrug and say good riddance.

Would anyone feel sorry for her? She furrowed her brow. Karine would. And maybe Paul from accounting. Perhaps even Sylvie from marketing, unless she was on meds again and not feeling anything at all.

But none of it really mattered.

What did matter was that the end of the world was upon her. Her personal, localized Armageddon had arrived in an innocent-looking envelope with the Energie NordSud logo on it.

Amanda grabbed her handbag and marched out the door. Keeping her back as straight as she could, she strode through the hallway, down the marble staircase, and out the main entrance.

*Eyes on the gate, one foot in front of the other.*

She nodded to the security guard and passed through the turnstile.

"Mademoiselle Roussel?" the guard asked, looking at his computer screen and then at her.

"Yes?"

"I must collect your access card."

"I'll come back next week to gather my things," she said as flatly as she could, handing him her card.

He nodded. "We'll let you in. Just make sure your visit is supervised by Monsieur Barre."

"Of course."

Amanda turned on her heel and marched away, hoping the guard hadn't seen her grimace. Truth was she'd rather donate her fine glass paperweight and Bodum French press to the company than ask Julien Barre—the bastard who'd fired her—to allow her to clean out her desk.

And have him breathe down her neck while she was doing it.

In the *métro* car, Amanda's eyebrows rose at the number of vacant seats before she remembered it was only three in the afternoon—the earliest she'd left the office in four years. As the train stations passed before her eyes, a plan formed in her mind. She'd get home and locate her father's Swiss Army knife. Then she'd down a few shots of vodka, return to the office, kill Julien, and kill herself.

It sounded like an excellent plan.

Twenty minutes later, she pushed open the door to her apartment and went straight to the minibar, praying she hadn't imagined the bottle of vodka hiding behind her expensive wines.

*Bingo!*

There it was—cold to the touch and as real as the sharp pain in her heart.

She filled a glass with the transparent liquid and drained it. The beverage burned her tongue. Amanda yelled out a battle cry, jumped up and down a few times while punching the air, and poured herself another glass. She set it on the coffee table and retrieved a tub of chocolate ice cream from the freezer. With her glass in one hand and the ice cream in the other, she kicked off her shoes and settled into her creamy leather sofa—the one she'd bought on credit, like almost everything else in her stylish little apartment.

By the time she finished her second glass, Amanda's diabolical plan had begun to lose its appeal. Julien Barre deserved to die, for sure, but murder was a messy business.

And suicide—even more so.

She pictured herself on the floor, blood gushing from her punctured stomach and trickling from her mouth.

*Ugh.*

Besides, what if she failed to finish Julien off? Or herself? After all, the biggest creature she'd ever assassinated had been a cockroach. The act had been so disgusting it gave her nightmares for weeks.

*Fine. No killing.*

But then what? She couldn't just sit here and do nothing—she was a fighter. Amanda clenched her fists and willed her vodka-soaked gray matter to hatch up a plan B. As soon as her brain obliged, she stomped to the bedroom and dug her crimson femme fatale lipstick from her makeup case. She shoved her most elegant evening gown, a tee, and a pair of panties into an overnight bag and rushed out of her apartment.

Plan B was insane, but it was carnage-free.

A few meters down the street, Amanda withdrew as much cash as the ATM would give her, and hailed a cab.

"Where to, *madame*?" the driver asked as she slumped into the backseat.

"Gare Saint-Lazare, please." She pulled out her phone and added on an impulse, "I'm going to Deauville."

"A beach weekend?" He smiled into the mirror.

"Nope. A night of gambling at the casino," she said, flashing him her brightest smile.

The driver's eyebrows shot up before he returned his gaze to the road. He didn't offer a comment.

Amanda sat back and tapped "blackjack rules" into the search engine on her phone.

She had three hours to master the game.

\* \* \*

By the time Amanda stepped into her hotel room, it was getting dark. She switched on the lights and surveyed her room.

*Nice.*

It had better be, considering the price she was paying for it. Royal Barrière was one of the town's best hotels, as grand and expensive as its name suggested. Was this reasonable? Certainly not. But tonight wasn't about reasonable. It was about winning big.

Besides, the thought of staying in a seedy hotel gave her goose bumps. She was no longer a discount-eligible, backpack-carrying student. She was twenty-eight—too old for seedy hotels. And, thankfully, not yet broke enough. Mind you, if everything went according to plan tonight, she wouldn't be broke at all.

The plan was simple, as all genius ideas were: exploit her beginner's luck.

Amanda was a gambling virgin, so new she still had her price tags. She'd never set foot in a casino or tried a slot machine. She'd never even played cards with friends.

Seeing as she had no friends.

She shook her head, brushing that thought away.

*I do have friends.* A whole bunch of them—because four counted as a bunch, right? And it was four more than she'd had ten years ago in her fat-padded, acne-decorated teens. Thank God, those days were gone. Now she was as slim, peach-skinned, and honey-blonde as the next self-respecting Parisian *it girl*. And, most importantly, she'd become the picture-perfect young lady her mother could parade in front of her friends.

As for Amanda's own friends, there was Karine, the PA from work who qualified thanks to the number of bitching sessions they'd shared over the years. Then there was Jeanne, a bartender, and Jeanne's fiancé, Mat, both of whom happened to be best friends with Amanda's ex. And finally, Patrick, business partner of said ex.

Amanda frowned at the annoying realization that three of her four friends were the legacy of her ex-boyfriend Rob.

*Note to self: diversify my social circle.*

She donned her strappy gown and refreshed her makeup. Then she grabbed her Chanel purse with her ID, cash, and the cocktail voucher the concierge had given her and headed to the famed Deauville Casino that adjoined her hotel.

Ten minutes into the game, Amanda began to suspect that her two-hour crash course on the train might have been insufficient. But it didn't matter because her beginner's luck should kick in any moment now.

She surveyed the players at her table to divert her mind from worrying.

*What a motley crew!*

Across from her sat an elderly Spanish couple. They wore matching T-shirts and smiled simultaneously, flashing their dentures. Next to them, two forty-something British women spoke to each other in an incomprehensible English dialect. A middle-aged Frenchman with greasy hair and darting eyes sat beside them. Amanda's neighbor to the left was a surgically enhanced bimbo of unknown provenance doused with a nauseating perfume and clad in a dress that was three sizes too small.

But the most remarkable person at the table was Amanda's neighbor to the right, whom she'd nicknamed Obsidian Eyes. In his late twenties, tall, swarthy, well built, and well dressed, the man was easy on the eyes. He wore a faux casual linen suit and played with the easy confidence of someone who knew what he was doing.

Amanda began to fidget with the strap of her watch, annoyed that the table blocked her view of his footwear. So many things could go wrong with the shoes! They could be synthetic or patent leather, have rubber soles, be coated in dirt or dust, sport pointy toes or toes that were too rounded . . . The list of potential offenses was long, and every one of them was unforgivable even with mitigating circumstances.

She was a bit of shoe fetishist.

Well, maybe a lot.

Overtaken by curiosity, Amanda discreetly pushed a card to the edge of the table until it fell to the floor. She bent down to pick it up and checked out the hunk's shoes so she could add him to her huge "discard" pile. But, to her surprise, Obsidian Eyes wore fine leather loafers that were flawless.

Probably Italian.

Handmade, without a doubt.

She sat up and studied his face again, perplexed. He had such fine eyes—intelligent and framed with extra thick lashes. The man was undeniably handsome, but not in a classic European way. Come to think of it, handsome wasn't the adjective she'd use to describe him. It didn't do him justice. It was too common, too weak. . . while he was kind of stunning.

His complexion and features held a touch of something exotic, faintly alien—something that kept her stealing glances at him whenever he turned his attention to his cards. Was it his wavy, jet-black hair, mesmerizing eyes, or chiseled jawline? Or maybe his exquisite eyebrows that made her think of a raven's wings? Whatever that *je ne sais quoi* was, it made him look more than ordinary. And hot.

The man was a blazing wildfire on legs.

As if his looks weren't enough, Obsidian Eyes played exceptionally well. Forty minutes into the game, his stacks of colorful chips had doubled while everyone else's—including Amanda's—had melted away.

That thought snapped her back into reality. Panicked, Amanda raised her eyes to the high ceiling of the casino.

*Please, I can't lose.*

She was gambling with her meager savings—half of it, to be exact. If the Supreme Being above intended to activate her beginner's luck, now was the time.

"Newbie?" Obsidian Eyes asked, his gaze never shifting from the deck in the dealer's hands.

He spoke French like a native. A slight Midi accent, maybe? A bit like Jeanne's, but less pronounced.

Amanda looked around, unsure whom he was talking to.

Obsidian Eyes finally lifted his gaze from the cards and gave her a panty-dropping smile.

She arched an eyebrow. "Does it show?"

"Mhmm."

*Ooh, that smile again.*

The dealer held up a card for her, and she started reaching for it when she noticed Obsidian Eyes give a quick shake of his head. She pulled back.

And won the hand.

"Thank you," she mouthed to her unexpected mentor.

He gave her a small nod.

She followed his discreet instructions for two more hands and won both. The evening was beginning to look up.

The dealer bowed and ceded his place to a good-looking young woman with sleek auburn hair smoothed back into the world's tightest bun.

She greeted the players and began to shuffle the cards.

Obsidian Eyes turned to Amanda. "Why blackjack? Beginners usually prefer the slots or roulette."

"I don't know . . .Too passive for me, I guess."

He nodded. "I avoid them, too."

"So you know what I mean."

"Yes. But that's not my only reason."

She cocked her head. "No?"

"The slots are twice as costly to players than the table games, and with roulette, too much depends on chance."

Amanda smirked. "Isn't that the case with all the games?"

"Not blackjack, if played right."

"Let me guess—*you* play it right."

He glanced at the dealer, who was engrossed in shuffling cards. "I know a trick or two."

One of the Brits stage-whispered to the other, "I hope he'll show me some of his tricks tonight." She paused before adding even louder, "In my room."

Both women burst out laughing.

Obsidian Eyes shifted uncomfortably and looked down at his hands, pretending he hadn't heard the saucy remark.

The man with greasy hair whispered something to the plastic bimbo.

She didn't acknowledge him. The woman was too busy multitasking. With her chest heaving, she stared at Obsidian Eyes and stroked her neck. Every five seconds she licked her lips and then pouted.

But the black-eyed hunk was oblivious to her onslaught. He turned to Amanda again. "I'm taking a break to stretch my legs."

"Er . . . OK."

He lowered his voice to a whisper. "I have a bad feeling about this dealer."

"Oh." She pushed her chips closer together like he had done and stood. "I'll do the same, then."

"What brings you to Deauville Casino tonight?" he asked as they strolled between the tables and observed the goings-on.

After a second's hesitation, she said, "I'm writing a book about gamblers."

"Participant observation, huh?"

Her eyebrows rose. "What do *you* know about participant observation?"

"Yeah, well, I need something to help me sleep when I get to my room at three in the morning." He shrugged. "Reading a few pages of *Tristes Tropiques* works better than any sleeping pill I've tried."

She giggled. "I'm passionate about cultural anthropology, but I could never finish that book."

"I like psychology books better," he said. "They're fun to read, and the info in them is useful in my trade."

"Oh?"

He nodded. "Especially books like Cialdini's *Influence* and the ones on how to read body language."

"I see."

"Hey, how about a glass of champagne on the terrace after I've won my target amount?" He gave her an innocent smile. A little too innocent.

"I have a cocktail voucher," she blurted before she could stop herself.

*Did I just accept his invitation?*

Oh, well. What harm could a drink do?

His face contorted in exaggerated disgust. "Trust me, you don't want their free cocktail unless you're a gustative masochist."

She put her hands on her hips. "I was given a free voucher, and I intend to use it."

"OK, OK. But don't say I didn't warn you."

She tilted her head to the side. "You said 'my target amount' earlier. Are you *that* good?"

"In all modesty . . . yes. But my target amount is also reasonable. And I have a spending threshold, too. When I reach it before I've won my target amount, I *always* stop."

"How very rational for a gambler!"

"I'm full of surprises, in case you haven't noticed." He gave her an appreciative look. "And I suspect that so are you, *ma belle*."

"When did I become your *belle*?"

"Oh, it's just a placeholder until you tell me your name."

*Should I?*

"So, what's your name, ma belle?"

"Am . . . elie. And yours?"

"Kes."

"What kind of name is Kes?"

"A Gypsy name."

"Like, a *real* Traveler Gypsy?"

"As authentic as they come."

"Ah." She raised her chin. "That explains it."

"Explains what, Amelie?"

"That you make me think of Tarzan."

"Really?"

"Not that you aren't dashing in your suit, but you look like someone who was born to ride horses bare-chested."

"Wow. You're the bluntest belle I've ever met."

"And you're the most gorgeous Gypsy I've ever met."

*Where did that come from? Must be the vodka.*

The corners of his mouth twitched. "So refreshingly honest. Why, I'm flattered."

She looked away.

*Honest, my foot.*

He wasn't just the most handsome Gypsy she'd ever seen—he was the most spectacular man, all ethnicities included.

*Now,* that *was honest.*

She turned to him and cleared her throat. "Shall we go back? Target amounts and all."

"Sure."

The sleek-haired dealer was leaving when they returned to their seats. Both giggling Brits and Greasy Hair were gone. The elderly couple and the bimbo still played, but judging by their dismal faces and the measly number of chips in front of them, they weren't doing well.

Kes had been right about the dealer.

"What does your gut tell you about this one?" Amanda eyed the middle-aged man who had taken over for his colleague.

"He's the best."

Her face fell.

Kes grinned. "Not for the house, ma belle, for us. Move closer so I can see your cards without twisting my neck."

She moved as close to him as their chairs allowed.

"Now relax and do exactly as I say."

Amanda glanced at Kes, but he had already turned his full attention to the cards.

\* \* \*

For the next hour, they played in near silence. The few times Amanda tried to strike up a conversation, Kes shushed her with a smile and a whispered "counting for two here, remember?"

And count he did.

Amanda's job was easy: she hit when he said hit, stood when he said stand, and split her cards when he said split. Their chip stacks kept growing until Kes laid his palms on the table and mouthed to her, *Stop.*

She gave him a puzzled look. "Now?"

He nodded and then tipped the dealer. "I'm going to call it a night."

"But we're winning. Please, you can't stop now."

"Oh yes, I can." He leaned to whisper in her ear, "And so should you before they ask us to back off. Besides, this deck is becoming too hot."

She hesitated. The seven hundred euros she'd won wasn't the amount she'd been hoping for when she jumped on the train at Saint-Lazare. It would hardly solve her problems . . . but it would pay her mortgage next month. In spite of the alcohol in her system, Amanda knew she would've lost half her savings tonight had it not been for Kes. Continuing to play without him would be unwise.

"What about that drink you promised me?" he asked.

"Sure." She stood and smoothed her dress. "Lead the way, maestro."

He took her to the bar where they climbed onto tall barstools and ordered their drinks. The voucher cocktail was as bad as Kes had predicted it would be. Amanda winced at its candy taste and pushed the glass away.

"How about a mojito?" Kes asked. "It's one of their more decent concoctions."

She nodded.

As he passed her the glass, their fingertips brushed.

Amanda couldn't help noting how pleasant that contact was. Actually, *pleasant* was an understatement. It was electrifying.

*Easy, girl. No one-night stands, remember?*

"So, what is it like, the life of a gambler?" she asked.

"I'm not a gambler. Well, not in the usual sense, anyway."

"Oh, yes?"

"I'm a card counter. I've made a decent living from it for five years."

"How old are you?"

"Twenty-six."

"So you see this as a job?"

He nodded. "That's exactly how I see it. I have a job that I like and am good at."

She felt a sharp pang at his words.

*Aren't you lucky?*

"What's wrong, Amelie?"

"Nothing." She gave him one of her fake smiles. "And what about five years ago—what was your occupation then? Palm-reading or playing the accordion in the métro?"

He smirked. "So tactful and unprejudiced. Have you applied for sainthood yet?"

"You didn't answer my question."

"If you were trying to imply those are common Gypsy occupations, you're wrong. At least, as far as the French *Gitans* are concerned."

She arched an eyebrow.

"Gitan men are typically itinerant vendors or metalworkers," he said. "My dad, for example, deals in scrap metal. Some are lumbermen. The women are usually artisans or peddlers. In the fall, everyone is a grape picker. We don't engage in the trades you mentioned."

"Oh, I didn't realize Gitans were the Gypsy elite. Please forgive my ignorance."

He moved a little closer and flashed her a toothy smile. "I see you're determined to insult me. But here's the thing—I'm not easily insulted."

"Is that so?"

"We Gypsies are a thick-skinned lot." He shrugged. "Can't afford to be touchy."

She blushed, suddenly embarrassed. Had she been too rude? She had, but not out of prejudice. Well, not only out of prejudice. She was trying to drive him away so she wouldn't have to make tough decisions when they finished their drinks.

Still, he didn't deserve her spite—he *had* just saved her from aggravating her already precarious financial situation.

"I was impressed with your memory and your mental arithmetic," she said, offering him the olive branch of a sincere compliment.

"At school, I was good at math."

"Did you go to college?"

He shook his head. "I hadn't even considered it."

"Why not?"

"For one, a college education isn't something my family believes in. And then . . . I stumbled on this book at a flea market when I was seventeen."

"What book?"

"*The Blackjack System.* I read it in one day, reread it three more times, and then practiced with my cousin."

"Couldn't you practice online?"

"I did that, too. But the system works only with a finite number of decks on the table and a human dealer."

"I see."

"I couldn't wait to turn eighteen so I could go to a casino and put my skills to the test."

"And it worked?"

"Not immediately, but with time I got better. You see, the beauty of blackjack is that luck isn't the decisive factor. Luck determines the cards you're dealt. But it's your knowledge and skill that determine how you play them."

"Are you really making money on this?" She narrowed her eyes. "Like, regularly?"

"I've made a good profit in almost every casino I've played in. Except the ones that figure out too quickly I'm counting cards."

"So what happens once Deauville Casino figures you out?"

"They'll ban me, and I'll move on to play elsewhere."

"And when every casino in France has banned you?"

"I'll play in Belgium, Switzerland, Italy, Germany, Spain, Portugal . . . Or I'll go to Vegas and then to Asia. The world is big."

"So that's your life plan?"

"You could say that."

She drained her mojito.

He beckoned to the bartender and then turned to Amanda. "Any food allergies or diet restrictions?"

"No. Why?"

"We'll have two cold cuts and cheese plates, please," he said to the barman.

When they swallowed the last slices of spicy chorizo, Kes asked matter-of-factly, "My hotel or yours?"

*Oh Lord.* There it was—decision time. But wait a minute. Why was she even considering it? She didn't do one-night stands. She wasn't that kind of girl. What she needed to do was wish him good night in her poshest accent and leave.

It was the only reasonable move.

Except . . . she wasn't being reasonable tonight. Right now, she was curious and thrilled. Her heart fluttered with anticipation. She all but drooled over the juicy exotic fruit that was this man. Just this once she itched to be wanton. After all, her reputation in that department was so unnaturally pristine it was begging for a stain.

And just like that, Amanda made up her mind: she was going to bed with Kes, the gambler she'd met a few hours ago.

He bit into his last pickle. "Do you have a boyfriend?"

"No. Do you?"

"Believe it or not, I've never had a boyfriend." His eyes crinkled with amusement. "I'm a virgin that way."

She chuckled.

He broke into an infectious grin before adding in a more serious tone, "No girlfriend at the moment, either."

"Do you have a condom?" she heard herself ask.

He blinked and then nodded. "Yep—in my room. My hotel then?"

"Only if it's decent."

"As decent as it gets in this town. I'm staying at Royal Barrière—it's the building next door."

Was his being at the same hotel as she was a sign, a green light of sorts? She could sneak out and go to her room as soon as the deed was done—a perfect setup for a hassle-free, controlled bit of fun. If she were ever going to have her first one-night stand, there wouldn't be a better occasion.

He must have seen the outcome of her expeditious debate on her face because he took her hand and led her from the bar.

*End of Excerpt*

# About the Author

Alix Nichols is an unapologetic caffeine addict and a longtime fan of Mr. Darcy, especially in his Colin Firth incarnation. She is the author of the bestselling Bistro La Bohème series.

At the age of six, she released her first romantic comedy. It featured highly creative spelling on a half dozen pages stitched together and bound in velvet paper.

Decades later, she still loves the romance genre. Her spelling has improved (somewhat), and her books have made Amazon Top 100 lists, climbing as high as #1. She lives in France with her family and their almost-human dog.

Connect with her online:

Blog: http://www.alixnichols.com
Facebook: www.facebook.com/AuthorAlixNichols
Twitter: twitter.com/aalix_nichols
Pinterest: http://www.pinterest.com/AuthorANichols
Goodreads: goodreads.com/alixnichols

Made in the USA
Middletown, DE
17 February 2017